MARSHLANDS
and
PROMETHEUS MISBOUND

ANDRÉ GIDE

MARSHLANDS

and

PROMETHEUS MISBOUND

Two Satires

Translated by
GEORGE D. PAINTER

A NEW DIRECTIONS BOOK

CONTENTS

MARSHLANDS

OR

THE TREATISE ON CONTINGENCY

Dic cur hic.

(The other school)

CONTENTS

*B*EFORE I EXPLAIN *my book to others, I am waiting for others to explain it to me. To explain it beforehand would be to restrict its meaning; for though we may know what we intended to say, we do not know if that was all we have actually been saying.—One always says more than just* THAT.—*And what interests me most in my book, is what I have put in without being aware of it—the part that belongs to the unconscious, which I should like to call, the part that belongs to God.—A book is always a collaboration, and the smaller the part of the Scribe, the more room there will be to welcome God, and the greater will be its value.—Let us await from everywhere the revelation of things; from the public, the revelation of our works.*

HUBERT

Towards five o'clock the day grew cooler; I shut my windows and went back to my writing.

At six o'clock in came my great friend Hubert; he was on his way from riding-school.

He said: "I say! Are you working?"

I replied: "I am writing *Marshlands*."

"And what is *Marshlands*?"   "A book."

"Would I like it?"   "No."

"Too clever?"   "Too boring."

"Why write it, then?"   "If I didn't, who would?"

"Still more confessions?"   "Hardly any."

"What then?"   "Sit down."

And when he had sat down, I said:

"I have read the following lines in Virgil:

> *Et tibi magna satis quamvis lapis omnia nudus*
> *Limosoque palus obducat pascua junco.*

Let me translate: a shepherd is talking to another shepherd; he tells him his field is, no doubt, full of stony ground and bogs, but it's good enough for him, and he is very happy to be contented with it.—No thought could be wiser, when a man cannot change his field, what do you say? . . ." Hubert said nothing. I proceeded:

15

"*Marshlands*, to particularize, is the story of one who cannot travel;—in Virgil his name is Tityrus;—*Marshlands* is the story of a man who, possessing the field of Tityrus, does not make any effort to leave it, but on the contrary is content to stay where he is. There—now I'll tell you the plot.—On the first day, he realizes he is contented, and reflects on what to do. On the second day a flight of migratory birds passes; in the morning he kills four widgeon, or teal, and towards evening he eats two of them, which he has cooked on a scanty fire of brushwood. He whiles away the third day by building a hut with some tall reeds. On the fourth day, he eats the two remaining widgeon. On the fifth day, he pulls down his hut, and tries to think of some more ingenious form of house. On the sixth day . . ."

"That'll do!" said Hubert, "I quite understand. You can go on writing, my dear fellow." And he left.

Night had fallen. I arranged my papers, and went out, without dining. Towards eight o'clock I arrived at Angela's flat.

Angela was still at table, in the middle of dessert. I sat down beside her, and began to peel her an orange. A servant brought in a tray of preserves, and when we were alone again Angela said, as she spread a slice of bread and butter for me: "What have you been doing to-day?"

I couldn't remember a single action, and replied, without thinking, "Nothing"; but then, to avoid possible digressions into psychology, I thought of my visitor, and cried: "My great friend Hubert came to see me at six o'clock."

"He has just left here," replied Angela, and took the opportunity to raise again a time-honoured subject for argument: "He at least does something," she said; "he makes use of his time."

Having said I had done nothing, I took offence at this. "Why, what does he do?" I asked . . . and she started off:

"He does heaps of things . . . to begin with, he rides . . . and then, you know perfectly well he is on the board of four industrial companies; and he runs yet another with his brother-in-law, for insurance against hail:—I have just taken out a policy. He goes to classes in popular biology, and gives public readings every Tuesday evening. He knows enough medicine to make himself useful in an emergency. Hubert does a great deal of good: five destitute families owe him their livelihood; he places workers who need work with employers who needed workers. He sends delicate children to sanatoria in the country. He has founded a workshop which employs blind boys in mending chairs. And lastly, on Sundays, he goes out shooting. But you! What do you do?"

"Well," I replied, in some embarrassment,—"I am writing *Marshlands*."

"*Marshlands*? What is that?" she said.

We had finished eating; I waited till we were in the drawing-room before replying.

When we had sat down by the fire, "*Marshlands*," I began, "is the story of a bachelor who lives in a tower entirely surrounded by marshes."

"Oh," she said.

"His name is Tityrus."

"What a frightful name," she said.

"Not at all," I replied, "—it is in Virgil. And anyway, I'm no good at inventing."

"But why a bachelor?"

"Oh! . . . just to simplify."

"Is that all?"

"No; I describe what he does."

"And what does he do?"

"He looks at the marshes. . . ."

"Why do you write?" she resumed, after a silence.

"Why do I write?—I don't know,—probably because writing is a form of action."

"You must read it to me," said Angela.

"Whenever you like. And it so happens that I have four or five pages in my pocket"; and taking them out immediately, I read, with all desirable lack of expression:

THE DIARY OF TITYRUS
OR
MARSHLANDS

"*FROM MY WINDOW I can see, if I raise my head a little, a garden which I have not as yet looked at with proper attention; to the right, a wood is shedding its leaves; beyond the garden, a level plain; to the left, a pond of which I shall speak again.*

"*The garden was sown, long ago, with hollyhocks and columbines, but my neglect has allowed the plants to run wild; because of the neighbouring pond, moss and rushes have encroached everywhere; the paths are overgrown with long grass; no place remains where I can still walk, except the long avenue leading from my room to the plain: I went along it one day when I decided to take a stroll. In the evening the animals that live in the wood cross the avenue on their way to drink at the pond; because of the twilight I can discern only dim grey shapes, and as night falls soon after, I never see them coming back.*"

"How that would have frightened me," said Angela; "—but please go on—it is extremely well-written."

I was feeling over-wrought by the effort of reading.

"Oh, that's really all there is," I told her; "the rest isn't finished."

"Then you have made notes," she cried—"oh, do read them! It's the most amusing part of all; they show what the author is trying to say much better than anything he will write afterwards."

So I continued, disappointed in advance, trying all the same to give my phrases an appearance of being unfinished.

"*From the windows of his tower Tityrus is able to fish with a line*—let me repeat, these are the merest notes . . .*"

"Do go on!"

"*Sad monotony of waiting for a bite, inadequacy of baits, multiplication of lines (symbolic)—inevitability of never catching anything.*"

"Why is that?"

"It's a symbolic truth."

"But supposing he did catch something?"

"Then it would be a different symbol and a different truth."

"But it's not a question of truth at all, since you arrange the facts to suit yourself."

"I arrange the facts in such a way as to make them conform to truth more closely than they do in real life; it's too complicated to explain now, but one must realize that the events are appropriate to the characters; that is what makes a good novel; nothing that ever happens to us would suit anyone else. If Hubert had been there, he would already have made a miraculous draught of fishes! Tityrus never gets a bite: it's a psychological truth."

"Well, yes—all right. Go on."

"*Prolongation below surface of the mosses on the bank. Indecision of reflections; pond-weeds; fish swimming by. When speaking of these, avoid calling them 'blank amazements.' *"

"I should hope not! But why make a note of that?"

19

"Because that is what my friend Hermogenes has already taken to calling carp."

"I don't think the expression is at all a happy one."

"Too bad. Shall I go on?"

"Yes, please. Your notes are most amusing."

"*At dawn Tityrus notices tall white cones rising on the plain. Salt-mines. He goes down to watch the work. A non-existent landscape; narrow embankments between two salt-marshes. Excessive whiteness of hoppers on sifting-machines (symbolic); impossible to look at them except in foggy weather; smoked-glass goggles protect the workers from eye-trouble.*

"*Tityrus puts a handful of salt in his pocket, and returns to his tower.*—That's all."

"Is it really?"

"All I've written so far."

"I'm afraid your story may be the least bit boring,"—said Angela.

An enormous silence ensued; after which I exclaimed, with much feeling: "Angela, Angela, I beg of you. When will you understand what it is that makes the subject of a book? What I want to express is the emotion my life has given me: the boredom, the emptiness, the mono-tony. I don't mind it myself, because I am writing *Marshlands*—but the life of Tityrus is a sheer nonentity; and our lives, Angela, I assure you, are even more colourless and mediocre."

"But I don't feel anything of the sort," said Angela.

"It's because you don't reflect upon it. And that is precisely the subject of my book. Tityrus is not dis-contented with his life; he enjoys looking at the marshes; a change in the weather gives them variety;—but just look at yourself! look at *your* story! How much variety is there in that! How long have you been living in this room? These cheap little flats!—and you're not the only one! Those windows looking on the street, or on back-yards; if you look out you see the opposite wall, or other people looking at you . . . But must I go on to make you ashamed of the dresses you wear—and do you really think we have ever managed to love each other?"

"Nine o'clock," she said; "this is the evening Hubert gives his reading, and you must allow me to go to it."

"What is he reading?" I couldn't help asking.

"You may be quite sure it won't be *Marshlands*!"—and away she went.

When I was home again I tried to put the opening of *Marshlands* into verse—I completed the first stanza:

> *When I gaze from my window*
> *Raising my head I see*
> *A small green wood that ne'er has known*
> *A day's festivity.*

And then I went to bed, for my day was over.

ANGELA

K EEP AN AGENDA; if I write down every day what
I have to do during the week, I shall order my time
wisely. In this way I decide my actions for myself; and
if I determine them in advance, without undue haste, I
am certain not to be dependent every morning on the
state of the weather. From my agenda I derive the
sentiment of duty; I write it a week ahead, in order to
have time to forget it, and to give myself surprises,
which are indispensable in my manner of life; in this
way I go to sleep every evening with a to-morrow before
me that is unknown, and yet already pre-ordained by
myself.

My agenda is divided into two parts: on one page I
write what I am going to do, and on the opposite page
I write every evening what I have done. Then I compare
the two; I subtract one from the other, and what I have
not done, or the deficit, becomes what I ought to have
done. I copy it out again every December, and this gives
me ideas full of moral significance.—I began it three
days ago.—For instance, this morning, opposite the
memorandum: try to get up at 6 o'clock, I wrote: got up
at 7—and then, in brackets: (negative surprise).—Next
on the agenda came various notes:

22

Write to Gustave and Leo.

Feel astonished at not having a letter from Julius.

Call on Gontran.

Think about Richard's personality.

Worry about the relationship between Hubert and Angela.

Try to find time to visit the Jardin des Plantes; study there the varieties of the lesser potamogeton for *Marshlands*.

Spend the evening at Angela's.

Then came the thought: (I write one for every day, in advance; they decide whether I am to be sad, or full of joy.)

"There are some things that one repeats every day, simply for want of anything better to do; it's not a matter of progress, nor even of keeping things going—but after all, one can't just do nothing at all. . . . This corresponds in time to the movement in space of caged animals, or of tides on the seashore."—I remember that this thought came to me when I was passing a restaurant with a terrace, and saw the waiters taking away one course and bringing in the next.—I wrote under it: "Good enough for *Marshlands*." And I prepared to think about Richard's personality. In a little writing-desk I keep my reflections and impressions on some of my best friends, one drawer to each. I took out the appropriate file and re-read:

RICHARD

SHEET I. Excellent person; merits all my esteem.

SHEET II. By unceasing application, has contrived to emerge from the complete destitution in which the death of his parents left him. His grandmother is still alive; he enfolds her in the pious and loving care which people so often feel for the aged; she lapsed into second childhood, however, many years ago. He married a woman poorer than himself, out of virtue, and makes her happy by remaining faithful to her.—Four children. I am godfather to a little girl who limps.

SHEET III. Richard had a very great veneration for my father; he is the most loyal of my friends. He is under the impression that he knows me completely, although he never reads anything I write; that is what makes it possible for me to write *Marshlands*; I think of him when I think of Tityrus; I would prefer never to have known him.—Angela and he have never met; they wouldn't be able to understand each other.

SHEET IV. Richard, to my misfortune, thinks very highly of me; this is the reason why I never dare do anything. It isn't easy to free oneself from another's esteem, so long as one continues to value it. Richard often tells me, with tears in his eyes, that I am incapable of a bad action, and this holds me back when, as sometimes happens, I would like to make up my mind to do something. What Richard admires in me is the passivity that keeps me in the paths of virtue into which others, of character like his, have pushed me. He often calls resignation a virtue, because that puts virtue within reach of the poor.

SHEET V. Works in an office all day. In the evening he sits with his wife and reads the paper, in order to be able to talk about something. "Have you seen Pailleron's new play at the Comédie Française?" he asked me the other day. He keeps up with all the latest arrivals. "Are you going to see the new gorillas?" he asks, when he hears I am going to the Jardin des Plantes. Richard treats me like a big child; I find it intolerable; he never takes anything I do seriously; very well then, I shall tell him the story of *Marshlands*.

SHEET VI. His wife's name is Ursula.

I took a Sheet VII and wrote:
"How horrible are all careers that do not profit a man—those, that is, which bring in nothing but money, and so little of that, that he always has to begin again without a pause. What utter stagnation! At the moment of death, what will they have accomplished?—They will have filled their place in life.—Yes, indeed! because they took one that was as small as themselves."

I don't mind it, because I'm writing *Marshlands*, otherwise I should think no better of myself than of them. But really, we must try to put a little variety into our existence.

At this moment my manservant brought in my refreshments and some letters,—including, as it happened, one from Julius, so I stopped feeling astonished at his silence;—I weighed myself, for the sake of hygiene, just as I would have done any other morning; I wrote a few sentences to Leo and Gustave; and then, while drinking my daily bowl of milk (as did some of the Lake-Poets), I thought:—'Hubert didn't understand *Marshlands* at all; he can't realize that, because an author doesn't write to instruct, he doesn't necessarily write to entertain. Tityrus bores him; he doesn't understand any position, unless it is a social position; he thinks he is different because he is busy—I must have explained myself badly. He thinks everything is for the best, because Tityrus is contented; but it is because Tityrus is contented that I want to stop being contented myself. What is needed, on the contrary, is indignation. I am going to make Tityrus despicable because of his resignation. . .'—I was on the point of beginning to think about Richard's personality again, when I heard the bell ring, and Richard himself, after sending up his card, came in. I was rather put out, as I find it difficult to think about people when they are actually present.

"Ah, my dear fellow!" I cried as I embraced him, "what a coincidence! I was going to think about you this very morning."

"I have come to ask a favour," he said "—oh, it's a mere nothing, but I thought, as you have nothing to do, you might be able to give me a few moments of your time. It's only a matter of a signature, an introduction; I need a sponsor; you will be my surety; I'll explain it all on the way; but we must hurry; I have to be at the office by ten o'clock."

I hate people to think I have nothing to do; so I replied: "Fortunately it is not quite nine, we shall just have time; but I myself have something to do at the Jardin des Plantes immediately after."

"Ah!" he began, "you are going to see the new . . ."

"No, my dear Richard," I interrupted, as it were casually, "—I am not going to see the gorillas. I have to go there to study some varieties of the lesser potamogeton for *Marshlands*."

My stupid answer immediately made me feel annoyed with Richard. Afraid of showing up our ignorance, he remained silent. "He ought to burst out laughing," I thought. "But he doesn't dare. I cannot endure his pity. Obviously he thinks me absurd. He hides his feelings from me, to prevent me from showing that mine are the same towards him. But each of us knows how the other feels. Our reciprocal esteem keeps its equilibrium because mine for him is propped against his for me; he dare not withdraw his, fearing that mine would fall with it. He shows me a patronizing affability. Ah! so much the worse for him; I'll tell him about *Marshlands*"—and I began by blandly asking: "How is your wife?"

Richard immediately went on by himself, without any help from me: "Ursula? Ah! poor dear! It's her eyes, now—she has strained them—it's her own fault. Shall I tell you, my dear fellow, what otherwise I would never have revealed to a soul?—But I know what a discreet friend you are.—Here is the whole story. Edward, my brother-in-law, was in urgent need of money; some had to be found somewhere. Ursula knew all about it, because her sister-in-law Jeanne came to see her the same day. Now I'd hardly a penny in the house, and we could only manage to pay the cook by stopping Albert's violin-lessons. I hated to do it, because they are the poor dear boy's only distraction during his long convalescence. I don't know how, but the cook had wind of it; the poor girl is very devoted to us;—you know her very well—Louise. She came to us in floods of tears, saying she would sooner go without food than distress Albert. Rather than hurt the good creature's feelings we had to accept; but I resolved then to get up two hours every night when my wife thought I was fast asleep, and work at some translations of English magazine articles, which I know how to place; in this way I hoped to scrape together the money of which we were depriving poor Louise.

"The first night all went well. Ursula was sound asleep. The second night I had hardly set to work, when who do you think walked in? Ursula!—She'd had the same idea: to pay Louise, she was making some little fire-screens, which she knows where to place;—you know she has a certain gift for water-colours . . . they're charming little objects, my dear fellow. . . . We were both very much moved; we kissed and shed tears. I tried in vain to persuade her to go back to bed—and she tires so easily you know—but she refused point-blank;— she begged me, as a tremendous proof of my affection, to let her stay and work beside me;—I had to consent, —but how tired she is getting! We do it every night now. It means losing a good deal of sleep—the only thing is, we've decided it's useless to go to bed in the first place, now we've stopped hiding it from each other."

"But what you have told me is extremely touching," I cried—and I thought to myself: "no, I shall never be able to tell him about *Marshlands*; on the contrary"— and I murmured: "Dear Richard, please believe that I understand your troubles perfectly—you really are terribly unhappy."

"No, my friend," he said, "I am not unhappy. Few things have been granted me, but with those few things I have built my happiness; do you think I have told you my story to move your pity? . . . With love and esteem all around me, with my work beside Ursula every evening . . . no, I would not change these joys for . . ."

There was a rather lengthy silence; at last I asked: "And the children?"

"Poor little souls!" he said, "that is what really makes me sad. What they ought to have is fresh air, out-door games, sunshine; they are wilting away in our narrow rooms. I don't mind it for myself, I am getting old; I am resigned to these things—but my children are de-jected, and it preys on my mind."

"It is true," I answered, "that your flat is rather stuffy —though if you open the window too wide all the smells of the street come in. Of course, there's always the Luxembourg Gardens. . . . In fact, that is the very subject of . . ." But I immediately thought: "No, decidedly I can't talk to him about *Marshlands*," and instead of finishing my remark I pretended to fall into a deep meditation.

After a short time I was on the point, from sheer desperation, of asking after his grandmother, when Richard signed to me that we had arrived.

"Hubert is already there," he said. "—To be sure, I haven't explained anything to you . . . I needed two guarantors—never mind,—you will understand—I'll get them to read you the documents."

"I think you two know each other,"—added Richard, as I shook hands with my great friend. He was already beginning with "Well! and how goes *Marshlands?*"—I gripped his hand more forcibly and said in a low voice: "Sh-sh! not now! you can follow me out, and then we'll talk."

As soon as the papers were signed, after taking leave of Richard, Hubert and I made off together.—As it happened, he had to go in the direction of the Jardin des Plantes for a class in practical obstetrics.

"Well," I began, "Here goes. You remember the widgeon; Tityrus had killed four, I told you. But no! he can't do it: shooting is forbidden. Just then, up comes a priest: the Church, he tells Tityrus, would have been much grieved to see him eating teal; such game is forbidden flesh; one can't be too careful; sin lurks for us everywhere; in case of doubt, abstinence is best; let us choose self-maceration;—the Church knows excellent forms of it, and of proved efficacity.—May I venture to advise a brother in the Lord? Eat, I beg of you, eat—mudworms.

"As soon as the priest departs, a doctor heaves in sight. You were about to eat teal! but didn't you know they are very dangerous! Malignant fevers are prevalent in these marshes; you must adapt your blood to your environment. *Similia similibus*, Tityrus, you know—like cures like! Eat mudworms (*Lumbriculi limosi*)—the very essence of the marshes is concentrated in them, and moreover they are a highly nutritious form of aliment."

"Faugh!" said Hubert.

"Yes, isn't it it repulsive?" I replied, "and the whole thing is frightfully bogus; as you may guess, all they are after is to preserve the game! But the most extraordinary thing is, that Tityrus tries the mudworms; after a few days he gets used to them, and soon he will find them delicious.—There now! isn't he revolting!?"

"He is a very happy man," said Hubert.

"Oh well, let's change the subject," I cried, losing patience. And remembering suddenly that I had to worry about the relationship between Hubert and Angela, I tried to induce him to talk.

"How monotonous it all is!" I began again, after a silence. "Nothing ever happens! We ought to try to stir up some activity in our lives. But one can't invent one's passions where they don't exist already!—Besides, I don't know anyone but Angela;—she and I have never fallen in love in any really decisive way:—whatever I may say to her this evening, I might just as well have said yesterday; we make no headway . . ."

Between each phrase I waited for him to speak. He kept silent. So I continued automatically: "I don't mind it for myself, because I am writing *Marshlands*—but what I find intolerable is that she doesn't realize this state of things exists. In fact that was what gave me the idea of writing *Marshlands*."

Hubert was roused at last: "—Why do you want to upset her, if she's happy as she is?"

"But she isn't happy, my dear fellow. She thinks she is, because she is unaware of her own condition; but you must admit that if blindness is added to mediocrity, it only makes it all the sadder."

"And supposing you opened her eyes; supposing you succeeded in making her unhappy?"

"To begin with, it would be much more interesting; she would at least stop being satisfied—she would start looking for something better."—But I was unable to get anything more out of him, for at this moment Hubert shrugged his shoulders and lapsed into silence.

After a minute he began again: "—I had no idea you knew Richard."

This was almost a question; I might have told him that Richard was Tityrus, but since, as far as I knew, Hubert had no right to despise Richard, I said simply: "He is a highly meritorious person." And I promised myself, by way of compensation, to talk about Richard to Angela that evening.

"Well, goodbye then," said Hubert, realizing that we wouldn't be saying anything more; "I'm in a hurry— you don't walk fast enough.—By the way, I shan't be able to come and see you this evening at six o'clock."

"Well, all the better," I answered; "it will make a change for us both."

He left me. I entered the garden alone, and took my unhurried way towards the plants. I am fond of this place; I come here often; all the gardeners know me; they let me into the sections that are closed to the public, and think me a man of science because, when I reach the ponds, I sit down. Thanks to constant supervision, these ponds remain in their natural state; they are fed noiselessly by running water. In them grow the plants that no one stops from growing, and multitudes of insects swim. I spend my time watching the insects; in fact that, in a way, is what gave me the idea of writing *Marshlands*; the feeling of an unprofitable contemplation, the emotion I have in the presence of delicate grey things.—That day I wrote the following for Tityrus:

More than all others, it is the wide, flat landscapes that attract me—the monotonous heaths—and I would have made long journeys in search of countrysides full of pools, were it not that I find them here all around me.—But do not think that I am sad; I am not even melancholy; I am Tityrus, and solitary, and I like a landscape, as I like a book, which does not distract me from my thoughts. For my thoughts are sad; they are serious, and, even when I am with other people, gloomy; I love my thoughts above all things else, and it is because I can wander there with them, that I seek level plains, unsmiling pools, and heaths. I wander gently with them there.

Why are my thoughts sad? If that sadness had made me suffer, I should have asked myself this question more frequently. If you had not pointed it out to me, I should not perhaps have known of its existence, for my thoughts often find amusement in a quantity of things that do not interest you in the least. For instance, they like re-reading these lines; they take joy in little tasks of which it would be useless to tell you, for you would not recognize any of them. . . .

A breeze was blowing that was almost warm; over the water leaned frail grasses, and the weight of insects made them bend. Thrusts of germination forced apart the flagstones that bordered the pool; a few drops of water escaped and moistened the roots of the plants. Mosses descended to the bottom of the pool, and gave it profundity with their shadow: glaucous water-weeds held bubbles of air for larvae to breathe. A water-beetle swam past. Unable to keep back a poetic thought, I took out another sheet of paper from my pocket, and wrote:

"Tityrus smiled."

After which, I felt hungry, and reserving for another day my study of the potamogetons, I made for the quay-side restaurant of which Peter had told me. I thought I should be alone, but I met Leo there, and he talked to me about Edgar. In the afternoon I called on various men of letters. About five o'clock a light shower of rain began to fall; I returned home; I wrote definitions of twenty nouns favoured by the modern school, and thought of as many as eight new epithets for the word *blastoderm*.

Towards evening I felt tired, and after dinner I went out to sleep at Angela's. I say at Angela's and not with Angela, because I have never gone further with her than trivial and innocuous substitutes.

She was alone. As I entered she was playing a Mozart sonatina with great precision on a newly-tuned piano. It was already late, and no other sound was to be heard. She had lit all the candles in all her candlesticks, and put on a dress with a small check pattern.

"Angela," I said as I came in, "we ought to try to put a little variety into our existence! Are you going to ask me again what I have been doing to-day?"

Evidently she did not quite understand the bitterness of what I had said, for she immediately asked:

"Very well then, what did you do to-day?"

Whereupon I answered, in spite of myself:

"I have seen my great friend Hubert."

"He has just left here," replied Angela.

"But my dear Angela," I cried, "can you never be at home to both of us at once?"

"Perhaps he is not so keen on the idea as all that," she said. "—But still, if *you* are, come to dinner on Friday evening. He will be there, and you can read us some poetry . . . By the way, have I invited you for to-morrow evening? I shall be at home to some men of letters; you are one of them.—I have asked them for nine o'clock."

"I have seen several to-day," I replied, meaning men of letters.—"I like the tranquil existence they lead. They are always at work, and yet one never seems to disturb them; when you go to see them, you'd think they were working only for your sake, and that they liked talking to you better still. Their little attentions are perfectly charming; they have plenty of leisure to think them out. I like these people because their life is ceaselessly occupied, and yet it is capable of being occupied with *us*. And as they never do anything worth while, one feels no remorse at taking up their time. But that reminds me: I have seen Tityrus."

"The bachelor?"

"Yes—but in real life he is married—a father of four. His name is Richard . . . don't tell me he has just left here, you don't know him."

And Angela, rather vexed, said: "There now, you see perfectly well that your story isn't true!"

"Not true, but why?—because there are six of them instead of one?—I've made Tityrus be alone in order to concentrate the monotony; it is an artistic device; surely you wouldn't have me make all six of them go fishing?"

"I am quite sure that in real life they all have different occupations!"

"If I described them, they would seem all too different;

if one uses actual events in a story, they never preserve the interrelated values they had in real life. To keep their truth one has to rearrange them. The important thing is, that I manifest the emotion they give me."

"But if that emotion is false?"

"Emotion, my dear, is never false. Have you never read that error begins when we form judgments? But why tell the same thing six times over?—since the impression they give is the same—yes, precisely, six times the same. . . . Would you like to know what they do—in real life?"

"Tell me, then," said Angela; "you seem annoyed."

"Not a bit of it," I cried. . . . "The father writes articles; the mother keeps house; there's a big boy who gives lessons, and a small one who takes them; the elder girl limps, and the other is too little, so she does nothing.— And then there's the cook. . . . The wife's name is Ursula. . . . And please notice that they all do exactly the same thing every day! ! !"

"Perhaps it's because they are poor," said Angela.

"Inevitably so!—But now do you understand *Marshlands*?—Richard, the moment he left school, lost his father,—a widower. He had to work; he was left very little money, and an elder brother took the lot; but to work at the most ridiculous jobs—just think!—those that bring in nothing but money!—in magazine-offices, copy at so much per page!—instead of travelling! He has seen nothing; his conversation has become insipid; he reads the papers to have something to talk about—when he has time—every hour of his day is taken up.—There's no chance of his ever being able to do anything else before he dies.—He has married a woman poorer than himself, out of sheer decency, not for love. Her name is Ursula—Oh! I've told you that already.—They have made of marriage a slow apprenticeship in love; they have come at last to love each other dearly, and to tell me about it. They love their children dearly, too, and their children love them dearly . . . and then there's the cook. On Sunday evening they all play lotto. . . . I nearly forgot the grandmother—she plays too, but as she can't see her cards, they whisper that she doesn't count. Oh! Angela! Richard! Everything in his life has been invented to stop up holes, to fill in gaping hiatuses,—everything! including his family. He was born a widower;—and every day there are the same lamentable second-bests, the same substitutes for all the best things.—And now, don't think ill of him,—he is extremely virtuous. Besides, he thinks himself happy."

"Why! If you aren't sobbing!" said Angela.

"Take no notice—it's nerves.—Angela, my dear friend,—don't you feel, taking it all in all, that our life is lacking in real adventure?"

"What can we do about it?" she replied gently, "—would you like us to take a little journey together? Look—Saturday—have you anything to do then?"

"But you can't really mean it, Angela—the day after to-morrow!"

"Why not? We could leave together early in the morning; you would have dined with me the night before—with Hubert; you could stay and sleep here . . . And now, good night," said Angela; "I'm going to bed. It's late and you've tired me rather. The maid has got your room ready."

"No, I won't stay, my dear,—forgive me, I am very excited. Before I go to bed, I have a great deal to write. Till to-morrow, then. I'm going home."

I wanted to consult my agenda. I left almost at a run, particularly as it was raining and I had no umbrella. As soon as I came in I wrote, for a date a week or two ahead, the following reflection, which did not refer solely to Richard:

"The virtue of the humble—acceptance; and it fits them so well, some of them, that one seems to realize that their life is made to the measure of their soul. Refrain, above all, from pitying them: their condition suits them; deplorable! They no longer notice mediocrity, so long as it's not mediocrity of fortune. What I said to Angela, although I was carried away, is true nevertheless; events happen to everyone in accordance with their appropriative affinities. Everybody finds what suits him. So if a man contents himself with the mediocrity he has, he proves that it fits him, and nothing else will happen. Destinies made to measure. Necessity of bursting one's clothes, just as the plane-tree or eucalyptus, as they grow, burst their bark."

"I'm writing far too much of this," I said to myself; "four words would have been enough.—But I don't like formulas. And now, let's examine this amazing proposition of Angela's."

I opened my agenda at the coming Saturday, and on the page for that day I read:

"Try to get up at six. Vary one's emotions.

—Write to Lucian and Charles.

—Find the equivalent of *nigra sed formosa* for Angela.

—Hope to be able to finish Darwin.

—Pay calls—on Laura (explain *Marshlands*), on Naomi, on Bernard, shatter Hubert (important).

—Towards evening try to go over the Pont de Solférino.

—Think of epithets for *fungosities*."

That was all. I took up my pen; I crossed everything out, and wrote in its place simply:

"Take a short pleasure-trip with Angela."

Then I went to bed.

THE SYMPOSIUM

THIS MORNING, AFTER a very restless night, I rose feeling rather unwell; instead of my bowl of milk I took, by way of variety, a little barley-water. In my agenda the page for the day was blank;—that meant: *Marshlands.* Such is my custom: I reserve for work the days when I haven't thought of doing anything else. I wrote all the morning. I wrote:

THE DIARY OF TITYRUS

"*I have crossed great heaths, vast plains, interminable expanses; even on the low hills the ground rose so little as to seem still asleep. I love wandering beside peat-bogs; paths have been made there, where the piled-up earth is less spongy and more solid. Everywhere else the ground is yielding, and the accumulation of mosses sinks beneath one's feet; the mosses are full of water, soft; hidden drainage, here and there, leaves them dry; and then heather grows on them, and a kind of dwarf pine; clubmosses (lycopodia) creep there; and the water is collected, at intervals, into dark, stagnant pools. I live in the lowlands, and care little to hoist myself on the hilltops, whence I know there is nothing new to be seen. I never gaze into the distance, although admittedly, the overcast sky has its charm.*

"*Sometimes, on the surface of the stagnant waters, there*

spreads a marvellous iridescence, and even the most beautiful butterflies have nothing on their wings to match it; this many-coloured film is formed of matter in a state of decomposition. Night on the pools awakes phosphorescences, and the will-o'-the-wisps that hover above them seem the sublimation of those same phosphorescences.

Marshes! what man could tell of your enchantments? Tityrus!"

"Let's not show these pages to Angela," I thought: "they would make Tityrus seem happy."

I also made the following notes:

"Tityrus buys an aquarium; he stands it in the centre of his greenest room, and rejoices in the idea that the entire landscape outside is summarized in it. He puts into it only mud and water; in the mud is a whole people of unknown creatures that manage their lives for his entertainment; in this ever-troubled water, where only things that come near the glass sides are visible, he enjoys the alternation of sunlight and shadow, that seems more brightly yellow there and more deeply grey—the lights that enter by the chinks in the closed shutters, and traverse the water.— Waters always more living than he had expected."

At this moment Richard came in; he invited me to lunch on Saturday. I was glad to be able to tell him that on precisely that day I had business out of town. He seemed very surprised and left without saying more.

I went out myself soon afterwards, when I had eaten my concise luncheon. I went to see Stephen, who was correcting the proofs of his play. He said it was very sensible of me to write *Marshlands*, because in his opinion I was by no means a born dramatist. I left him. In the street I ran into Roland, who accompanied me to Abel's. There I found Claudius and Urbanus, the poets; they were engaged in averring that it was no longer possible to write plays; each disagreed with the reasons the other gave for this, but they were of one accord in suppressing the theatre. They also said that I did well to give up writing poetry, as I was not very successful at it. Theodore came in, and then Walter, whom I can't abide. I left, and Roland came out with me. As soon as we reached the street I began:

"What an insufferable existence! Can you bear it, my dear fellow?"

"Yes, well enough," he replied—"but why 'insufferable'?"

"It's enough that it might be different, and isn't. All our acts are so well-known that a substitute could do them for us, and by repeating our words of yesterday, coin our phrases of to-morrow. Thursday is Abel's day for being at home; he would have been as much astonished at not seeing Urbanus, Claudius, Walter and you come in, as we all should have been, if we hadn't found him at home. Oh! don't think I'm complaining for my own sake; but I couldn't stand it any longer:—I'm leaving—I'm leaving on a journey."

"You?" said Roland. "Pooh! where, and when?"

"The day after to-morrow—where? I don't know . . . but you must understand, my dear fellow, that if I knew where I was going, and what I'm to do when I get there, it would not take me out of my suffering. I am leaving simply for the sake of leaving; the very surprise of it is my goal—the unforeseen—do you take my meaning?— the unforeseen! I don't suggest that you should come with me, because I'm taking Angela—but why don't you go away yourself, you too, on your own account, no matter where, and leave these incurables to stagnate?"

"Excuse me," said Roland, "I am not like you; when I set out, I like to know where I'm going."

"Very well, in that case one has to choose! What shall I suggest?—Africa! Do you know Biskra? Think of the sunlight on the sands! and the palmtrees. Roland! Roland! The dromedaries!—Remember that this very sun, that seems so pitiable when we glimpse it between the rooftops, behind the city and its dust, shines already, already shines over there; remember that everything is everywhere available! Will you always sit and wait? Ah! Roland! It is lack of air here, as much as boredom, that makes us yawn; will you go?"

"My dear fellow," said Roland, "it may well be that the most delightful surprises await me over there;—but there are too many responsibilities that hold me back—I prefer not to harbour useless desires. I cannot go to Biskra."

"But the whole idea," I replied, "is, precisely, to leave these responsibilities that have you in their hold.—Do you mean to accept being tied to them for ever? It makes no difference to me, you understand, because I am leaving for a different journey;—but remember, perhaps we only live once, and how small is the circle in which you are tethered!"

"Ah, my dear fellow," he said, "insist no more—I have very important reasons, and your argumentation wearies me. I cannot go to Biskra."

"Then let's leave it at that—" I said; "besides, here's where I live,—well! goodbye for some time to come—and, if you would be so kind, please inform all the others of my departure."

I went in.

At six o'clock in came my great friend Hubert; he was on his way back from a business committee-meeting. He said:

"They've been talking to me about *Marshlands*!"

"Who's they?" I asked, much excited.

"Friends. . . . You know, they don't care for it much; someone even said to me that you would do better to write something else."

"Then don't tell me about it."

"You know," he went on, "I'm not well up in these things; I'm only a listener; so long as it amuses you to write *Marshlands*. . . ."

"But it doesn't amuse me at all," I cried; "I'm writing *Marshlands* because . . . anyway, let's talk about something else. . . . I'm leaving on a journey."

"Pooh!" exclaimed Hubert.

"Yes," said I, "one needs to get out of town for a while, now and then. I'm leaving the day after to-morrow; and I don't know where for. . . . I'm taking Angela."

"What, at your age!"

"But, my dear fellow, it was she who asked me. I don't suggest that you should come with us, because I know you are very busy. . . ."

"And besides, you prefer to be alone together. Good enough. Will you be away for long?"

"Not too long; time and money limit us; but the important thing is to get away from Paris; one can only leave a city by energetic methods, such as express-trains; the difficulty is, to get past the suburbs." I stood up to walk about and increase my excitement: "How many stations there are, before the real country! At each one, people alight; it's as if they fell at the very beginning of the race; the carriages gradually empty.—Travellers! where are the travellers?—Those who still remain are on business; and the stokers and engine-drivers, who go to the very end, stay in their engines. Besides, even at the end, there is another town.—Countrysides! Where are the countrysides?"

"My dear fellow," said Hubert, himself getting up

and walking about, "you exaggerate: countrysides begin where towns leave off, it's perfectly simple."

I went on:

"But, my dear fellow, that's just it, towns don't leave off; and then, when they do, it's the suburbs . . . You seem to forget the suburbs—everything, that is, that lies between two towns. Smaller houses, with greater spaces between them, something still uglier than the town . . . pieces of town spun out; vegetable-gardens! And embankments bordering the road. The road! you have to keep to it, everyone must, and you can't go anywhere else. . . ."

"You ought to put that into *Marshlands*," said Hubert.

At this I became really annoyed:

"Can it be, my poor friend, that you have never understood anything about the reasons for a poem's existence—its nature—how it comes into being? A book . . . but, Hubert, a book is tight, full, smooth as an egg. One couldn't get anything else into it, not so much as a pinpoint, except by force, and its form would be smashed to pieces."

"Then your egg is full?" replied Hubert.

"But, my dear fellow," I cried, "one doesn't fill an egg: eggs are born full . . . Besides, that is already in *Marshlands* . . . and anyway it seems to me stupid to say that I should do better to write something else . . . stupid! do you hear? . . . Something else, indeed! Why, nothing would suit me better; but do try to understand that here, too, there are embankments on either side: our roads are forced, so is our labour, and so are our works. I take my position here because no one has taken it before me; I choose a subject by process of elimination, and I choose *Marshlands* because I am quite certain that no one will be found so destitute as to come and work on my land;

that is what I tried to express by these words: *I am Tityrus, and I am alone.*—I have read that to you, but you didn't take any notice . . . And then, how many times have I begged you never to talk to me about literature! By the way—" I continued, in order to change the subject "—will you be going to Angela's this evening? She's having an 'at home'."

"For men of letters . . . No," he answered, "as you know, I don't like these over-crowded parties where one does nothing but talk; and I thought you too felt stifled in them."

"That's true," I went on, "but I don't want to disoblige Angela; she has asked me specially. Besides, I want to see Hamilcar there, to point out to him that it's stifling. Angela's drawing-room is much too small for evening-parties; I shall endeavour to tell her so; I shall even use the word *exiguous*; and then I want to talk to Martin."

"As you like," said Hubert, "but I must leave you; goodbye."

He went.

I put my papers in order; I dined; as I ate, I thought about the journey; I repeated to myself: "Only one more day!"—Towards the end of the meal I felt myself so overcome by Angela's proposal, that I thought it my duty to write her the following words: '*Perception begins where sensation changes; hence the necessity for travel.*' Then, as soon as the letter was in its envelope, I took my docile way to her house.

Angela lives on the fourth floor.

On her at-home days, Angela puts a bench in front of her door, and another on the second landing by Laura's door; one pauses there to recover breath; one prepares for lack of air; these are stations in the dolorous way up; so I sat down, out of breath, on the first bench, and taking a sheet of paper out of my pocket, I tried to formulate arguments for Martin's benefit. I wrote:

'One doesn't go out; it's a mistake not to. It's true that one can't; but that is because one doesn't.—No! that's not right. Let's begin again. I tore it up. What has to be pointed out is, that each of us, though shut in, thinks himself out of doors. Woe is me! Think of an example.—At this moment someone came up the stairs; it was Martin. He said:

"I say! Are you working?"

I replied:

"My dear fellow, good evening. I am in the middle of writing to you; do not disturb me. You can wait for me upstairs on the bench."

He went up.

I wrote:

"One doesn't go out;—and it's a mistake not to. It's true that one can't; but that is because one doesn't.—One doesn't because one thinks oneself already outside. If one was aware of being shut in, one would at least feel the desire to go out."

—No! that's not right! That's not it! Let's begin again. I tore it up.—What has to be pointed out is, that each of us thinks he is outside because he doesn't trouble to look.—Moreover, he doesn't look because he is blind. Woe is me! I can't make head or tail of it . . . But then, this is a horribly inconvenient place for production.—I took out another sheet.—At this moment someone came up the stairs; it was Alexander, the philosopher. He said:

"I say! Are you working?"

I replied, absorbed in my task:

"Good evening. I am writing to Martin. He is upstairs

on the bench.—Sit down. I've nearly finished . . . Oh!
isn't there any room left? . . ."

"It doesn't matter," said Alexander, "as I have my
shooting stick." And unfolding his gadget, he sat down
and waited.

"There, I've finished," I answered. And leaning
over the banisters: "Martin!" I cried, "are you up
there?"

"Yes!" he shouted. "I'm waiting. Bring your bench
with you."

So, as at Angela's I'm practically in my own home, I
lugged my seat upstairs; and there, when all three of us
were settled down, Martin and I exchanged sheets, while
Alexander waited.

On my sheet was written:

*Being blind in order to believe oneself happy. Believing one
sees clearly in order not to try to see at all, because:*

One can only see one's unhappiness.

On his sheet was written:

*Being happy in one's blindness. Believing one sees clearly in
order not to try to see at all, because:*

One can only be unhappy at seeing oneself.

"But," I cried, "it's precisely what you rejoice in,
that I deplore. And it must be I that am in the right,
since I deplore that you should rejoice in it, while you
can't very well rejoice that I should deplore it.—Let's
begin again."

Alexander was still waiting.

"It's nearly finished," I said to him,"—we'll explain to
you afterwards."

We each took back our sheets.

I wrote: "*You remind me of people who translate* 'Numero
Deus impare gaudet' *by*: 'The Number Deuce delights in
being odd,' *and think it is perfectly right.—Now if it were*

46

true that oddness carries with it any promise of wellbeing—I mean, of liberty, one ought to say to Number Deuce:

"But, my poor friend, odd is just what you are not; if you wish to derive pleasure from being so, do at least try to become so."

He wrote:

"You remind me of people who translate 'Et dona ferentes' *by*: 'I fear the Greeks'—*and then don't notice the gifts.— Now, if it were true that every gift hides a Greek who immediately afterwards takes us prisoner;—I would say to the Greek:* 'Gentle Greek, give and take; then we shall be quits. I am your man, it's true, but without that you wouldn't have given me anything.' *Where I say Greek, understand Necessity. For she takes only as much as she gives."*

We exchanged sheets. A short time elapsed.

At the bottom of my sheet, he wrote:

"The more I reflect upon it, the more stupid I find your example, because after all . . ."

At the bottom of his sheet I wrote: *"The more I reflect upon it, the more stupid I find your example, because after all . . ."*

. . . Here, as each sheet was full, we both turned over —but on the verso of his could already be read:

—On the happiness of keeping to rule. Being joyful. The quest for a typical menu.

1. *Soup (à la Monsieur Huysmans);*
2. *Beefsteak (à la Monsieur Barrès);*
3. *Choice of vegetables (à la Monsieur Gabriel Trarieux);*
4. *Magnum of Évian water (à la Monsieur Mallarmé);*
5. *Greenery-yallery Chartreuse (à la Monsieur Oscar Wilde).*

On my sheet could be read simply my poetic thought in the Jardin des Plantes:

"Tityrus smiled."

47

Martin said: "Who's Tityrus?"

I replied: "He's myself."

—"Then you do smile sometimes!" he went on.

—"But my dear fellow, give me a chance to explain;—
(this is what comes of letting oneself go! . . .) Tityrus is
me, and he isn't me;—Tityrus is the imbecile; he's me,
he's you—he's all of us. . . . And please don't giggle
like that—it's most annoying;—I take imbecile in the
sense of infirm; the thought of his misery is not always
present to him; that's what I was saying just now. We
all have our moments of self-forgetfulness; but do please
understand that the expression you have there was
nothing but a poetic thought. . . ."

Alexander was reading our papers. Alexander is a
philosopher; of what he says I always feel mistrustful,
and to it I never make answer.—He smiled, and turning
towards me, began:

—"It seems to me, dear sir, that what you call a 'free
act' would be, according to you, an act dependent on
nothing; follow me: detachable—note my train of
reasoning: omissible,—and my conclusion: valueless.
Re-attach yourself to everything, dear sir, and do not
ask for contingency; in the first place, you would not get
it, and if you did, what would it profit you?"

I said nothing, as is my custom; when a philosopher
answers you, you no longer understand in the least what
it was you had asked him.—People could be heard
climbing the stairs; it was Clement, Prosper and Casimir.
—"So then," said they, seeing Alexander settled down
with us—"You have become stoics?—Please to enter,
Gentlemen of the Portico."

Their witticism seemed to me pretentious, so much so
that I felt it my duty not to go in until they had preceded me.

Angela's drawing-room was already full of people; in the middle of them all Angela was circulating, smiling, offering coffee and buns. As soon as she saw me she hurried up:

"Oh! There you are," she said, *sotto voce*; "I'm rather afraid they are getting bored; you must recite us some verses."

"But," I replied, "they won't be any the less bored,—and besides, you know I don't know any."

"But you do, you do; you've always just written something or other."

At this moment Hildebrand approached.

"Ah! dear sir," said he, taking my hand,"—delighted to see you. I haven't had the pleasure of reading your latest work, but my friend Hubert has told me great things of it. . . . And it seems that this evening you are going to do us the favour of reading us some verses. . . . "

Angela had eclipsed herself.

Ildevert loomed up:

"So, my dear sir," said he, "you are writing *Marshlands*?"

"How did you know?" I cried.

"But," he went on (exaggerating)—"nobody talks of anything else;—and it seems, moreover, that it will bear no resemblance to your last work—which I haven't had the pleasure of reading, but my friend Hubert has talked to me a great deal about it.—You are going to read us some lines, are you not?"

"Not fishing-lines, I suppose," said Isidore fatuously "—it seems *Marshlands* is full of them,—or so Hubert says. Oh, by the way, my dear fellow,—what *is* *Marshlands*?"

Valentine drew near, and as several persons were all listening together, I became confused.

"*Marshlands*," I began, "is the story of the neutral ground which belongs to everybody . . . —or, to put it better, it's about the normal man, the foundation on which everyone begins—it's the story of the third person, he of whom one speaks,—who lives in each of us, but dies not when we die.—In Virgil he is called Tityrus— and we are expressly told that he is *lying down*—"*Tityre recubans*." *Marshlands* is the story of the man who lies down."

"I say," said Patras, "—I thought it was the story of a bog."

"Sir," said I, "opinions differ, the essence endures.— Try to understand, I beg of you, that the only way of telling the same thing to everyone—I say, mark you, the same thing, is to change its form to suit each new mind that receives it.—At the present moment, *Marshlands* is the story of Angela's drawing-room."

"In fact, I can see you haven't quite made up your mind yet," said Anatole.

Philoxenus came up.

"Sir," said he, "everyone is waiting for your verses."

"Shush! Shush!" exclaimed Angela; "—he is just going to recite."

Everyone stopped talking.

"But, gentlemen," I cried, exasperated, "I assure you I have nothing worth hearing. Rather than disoblige you, I shall be forced to read you quite a small piece, which has no . . ."

"Read it! Read it!" said several voices.

"Very well, gentlemen, if you insist. . . ."

I drew a page from my pocket, and without taking up an attitude, I read from it in an expressionless manner:

A WALK

We took our walk through heathy land.
If only God would understand!
We wandered on through heathy land,
And when dusk fell and darkened it,
We felt that we would like to sit,
Because we were too tired to stand.

Everyone continued to keep silence; evidently they didn't understand that was the end; they were still waiting.

"That is the end," I said.

Then, amid the lull, the voice of Angela was heard; "Ah! Charming!—You ought to put that into *Marshlands*." And as they all still remained silent:—"Don't you agree, gentlemen, that he ought to put that into *Marshlands*?"

Then, for a few instants, there was a kind of uproar, for some kept asking: "*Marshlands? Marshlands?* What's that?"—and the others explained what *Marshlands* was, but in a way that didn't seem as yet to be very certain.

I couldn't get in a word, but at this moment, the physiologist Carolus, with his mania for going to primary sources, came up to me, with an air of interrogation.

"*Marshlands?*" I began immediately. "Sir, it is about animals who live in dark caves, who lose their sight from not making use of it.—And now let me be, I feel terribly hot."

Nevertheless, Evaristus, the shrewd critic, argued: "I'm afraid, as a subject, that may be a little too special."

"But, sir," I had to say, "there's no such thing as a subject that is too particular. *Et tibi magna satis*, wrote Virgil, and that, precisely, is my subject—much as I deplore it. Art consists in depicting a particular subject with sufficient power for the generality on which it depended to be comprehended in it. This can only be expressed very badly in abstract terms, because it is itself an abstract thought—but you will, assuredly, take my meaning, if you think of all the enormous landscape that passes through a keyhole, as soon as the eye gets near enough to the door. A person who sees nothing there but a keyhole, would see the whole world through it, if only he thought of bending down. It is enough that there should be the possibility of generalization; to make that generalization is the part of the reader, the critic."

"Sir," said he, "you facilitate your task to a singular degree."

"And if not, I suppress yours," I replied, gasping. He withdrew. "Ah!" I thought, "now I shall be able to get my breath again!"

But, precisely at that moment, Angela took me by the sleeve.

"Come here," she said, "I have something to show you."

And pulling me near to the curtain, she raised it discreetly, so that I was able to see on the window-pane a big black blob that was making a noise.

"So that you wouldn't be able to complain of the heat, I have had a ventilator put in," said she.

"Ah! my dear Angela!"

"The only thing is," she went on, "that as it made a noise, I've had to keep the curtain drawn over it."

"Oh! So that's what it is! But, my dear, it is much too small!"

"The man at the shop told me it was the model for men of letters. The larger size was for political meetings, but then we shouldn't have been able to hear ourselves speak."

At this moment Barnaby, the moralist, came and pulled me by the sleeve, and said:

"Various friends of yours have told me enough about *Marshlands* for me to see quite clearly what you are trying to do; I have come to warn you that to me it seems useless and offensive. You want to force people to act because you have a horror of stagnation—to force them to act, without considering that the more you intervene, prior to their acts, the less those acts result from them. Your responsibility is thereby increased; theirs is proportionately diminished. Now it is the responsibility for acts, and that alone, that gives them their importance in our eyes—and their appearance is nothing. You can never teach people to will: *velle non discitur*; you merely influence them; much good will it do then, if you succeed at last in endorsing a few worthless deeds!"

I said to him:

"You maintain then, sir, that we should disinterest ourselves in others, since you deny that we can make them our business."

"At least, it is very difficult so to busy ourselves, and our function, we who do so, is not to engender great acts, with more or less mediation, but to make the responsibility for small ones greater and greater."

"You mean, to increase people's fear of action? It's not responsibilities that you will enlarge, but scruples. In this way you reduce the field of liberty still further. The really responsible act is the free act; our acts are free no longer; what I want is not to generate action, but to disengage freedom. . . ."

Then he smiled subtly to give point to what he was about to say; which was:

"So then—if I take your meaning correctly, sir—you wish to constrain people to freedom. . . ."

"Sir," I cried, "when I see people about me who are sick, I feel anxious—and if I do not seek to cure them, for fear, as you would say, of diminishing the value of their cure, at least I try to show them that they are sick—and to tell them so."

Galeas approached, solely in order to edge in this ineptitude:

"It's not by showing a sick man his sickness that you can cure him, but by showing him the spectacle of health. They ought to hang a painting of a normal man over every hospital-bed, and cram the corridors with statues of the Farnese Hercules."

Then Valentine intervened and said:

"In the first place, the normal man's name isn't Hercules. . . ." Immediately everyone exclaimed "Shush! Shush! The great Valentine Knox is going to speak."

He went on:

"Health doesn't seem to me so enviable a blessing as all that. It is only a state of equilibrium, a mediocrity in all things; it is the absence of hypertrophies. Our value consists only in that which distinguishes us from others; our idiosyncracy is the sickness that gives us value;—or, in other terms: our importance lies in what we alone possess, what can't be found in anyone else, what this *normal man* of yours has not,—in fact, what you call sickness.

"You must cease henceforth to look upon *sickness* as a lack; on the contrary, it is something extra; a hunchback is a man plus a hump, and I would prefer you to regard health as a lack of sickness.

"The *normal man* is of little importance to us; I would venture to say that he can be dispensed with—for one finds him everywhere. He is the highest common factor of humanity, the factor which, in mathematics, given a set of numbers, you can remove from each without depriving them of their *individual value*. The *normal man* (this expression exasperates me) is the residue, the dross which, after the fusion that vaporizes particularities, one finds at the bottom of the crucible. He is the primeval pigeon which one reconstitutes after crossing rare varieties—a grey pigeon—his colour-feathers have all dropped away, and there is nothing left to distinguish him."

I, seized with enthusiasm because he spoke about grey pigeons, wanted to shake him by the hand, and I exclaimed:

"Ah! Mr. Valentine!"

He said simply: "Man of letters, be silent. In the first place, I am only interested in madmen, and you are appallingly sensible." Then he continued: "The normal man is the person I met in the street and called by my name, mistaking him at first for myself; I held out my hand to him and cried: 'My poor Knox, how off-colour you look to-day! And what has become of your monocle?' And what surprised me was that Roland, who was walking with me, also called him by *his* name, and said to him simultaneously with me: 'Poor Roland! And where have you left your beard?' And then, as the fellow bored us, we suppressed him, without remorse, because he had nothing new to offer. Besides, he didn't say a word, for he was a pitiable creature. Do you know who he is, this normal man: he is the third person, he of whom one speaks . . ."

He turned towards me; and I turned to Ildevert and Isidore, and said to them:

"There! What did I tell you?"

Valentine continued, very loudly, fixing his eyes on me: "In Virgil his name is Tityrus; he dies not when we

die, and lives on everybody else."—and he added, roaring
with laughter, at my expense: "And that's why it doesn't
much matter if one kills him." And Ildevert and Isidore
held their sides too, and cried:

"In that case, sir, suppress Tityrus!"

Then, unable to hold out any longer, exasperated, I
exclaimed in my turn:

"Hush! Quiet! Listen to me!" And I began at random:

"Yes, gentlemen, yes! Tityrus has his sickness! ! !—
All of us, yes! all of us have, and throughout our lives,
as in those periods of depression when the mania of doubt
takes hold of us:—did we turn the key in the lock to-
night? we go and look; did we put our tie on this morning? we finger our collar; did we button our trousers, this
evening? we make sure. There! look at Madrus, who still
wasn't quite happy about it! And Borace!—You see I'm
right. And mark that we knew we'd done the thing
perfectly;—we do it again because we are sick—of the
malady of retrospection. We do it again because we've
done it already; each of our acts of yesterday seems to
call upon us to-day; it's like a child to whom we've
given life, and for whom henceforth we have to provide a
living . . ."

I was worn out, and could hear that I was expressing
myself badly . . .

"Whenever we start something, we feel we ought to
keep it going; hence our fear of too much action, lest it
should make us too dependent—for each act, instead of
becoming, once we've performed it, a taking-off point,
becomes the hollow bed on which we fall back—
recubans."

"What you're saying now is rather interesting," began
Pontius . . .

"No, sir, it isn't interesting at all—and I oughtn't on

any account to put it into *Marshlands* . . . I was saying that our personality is no longer separable from the manner in which we act—it consists in the act itself—in the two acts that we perform (like a trill in music)—or at most three. Who is Bernard? He is the person who is seen on Thursdays at Octavius's.—Who is Octavius? He is the person who is at home on Thursdays to Bernard. —What else? He is the person who goes on Mondays to Bernard's—Who is . . . but who are we all, gentlemen? We are the people who go every Friday evening to Angela's."

"But, sir," said Lucian, out of politeness, "in the first place, so much the better for us; and then, you can be sure that is our only point of contact!"

"Eh! only too true, dear sir," I went on, "I realize perfectly that when Hubert comes to see me every day at six o'clock, he can't be with you at the same time; but what difference does it make, if the person whom you are at home to every day is Bridget?—What does it matter, even, if Joachim only sees her every other day?— Do you think I'm drawing up statistics?—No! but I'd rather walk *to-day* on my hands, than walk on my feet— *as I did yesterday!*"

"Still, it seems to me that that is what you are doing," said Tullius stupidly.

"But, sir, that is precisely what I'm complaining about; please notice that I said "I'd rather"! Besides, if I tried to do it now, in the street, they'd shut me up for being out of my mind. And that's exactly what provokes me—the fact that everything external, laws, morality, pavements, should seem to determine our relapses and take upon itself our monotony,—when everything, at bottom, harmonizes so perfectly with our love of repetition."

"Then what are you complaining of?" exclaimed Tancred and Gaspard.

"Why, precisely, of the fact that no one complains! Accepting the evil aggravates it,—it becomes vice, gentlemen, since in the end we come to enjoy it. What I complain of, sir, is that we don't kick against the pricks; that we have every appearance of dining well when we're eating hash, and look perfectly satisfied after a meal worth fourpence. I complain that we don't revolt against . . ."

"Oh! Oh! Oh!" cried several—"so you're a revolutionary now?"

"But not at all, gentlemen, I'm nothing of the sort. Revolutionary, indeed! you won't let me finish,—I mean that we don't revolt . . . inwardly. It's not of the distribution of property that I complain; it's of ourselves; it's of our morals. . . ."

"Really, sir," cried an uproar of voices—"you reproach people with living as they do,—and then you deny their ability to live otherwise, and you reproach them with being contented to live like that—but if they like it—but . . . but really, sir: what-in-heaven's-name-do-you-want? ? ?"

I was bathed in perspiration, and completely flurried; I replied distraughtly:

"What do I want? Gentlemen, what I want—I, personally—is to finish *Marshlands*."

Then Nicodemus darted out of the group and came to shake my hand, shouting:

"Ah! Sir, what a good deed that will be!" All the others had immediately turned their backs.

"Why," I said, "do you know it?"

"No, sir," he answered, "but my friend Hubert has told me a great deal about it."

"Ah! he has told you. . . ."

"Yes, sir, about the fisherman who finds mudworms so delicious that he eats them instead of baiting his lines with them—and then he doesn't catch anything . . . naturally. I find that very comical!"

He had understood nothing.—I must begin everything all over again. Oh! I am worn out! And to think that's the very thing I would like to make them understand, that one must begin again—always—begin again to make people understand; how perplexing it is; I can't go on; ah! I've already said that. . . .

And as at Angela's I am practically in my own house, I went up to her, took out my watch, and shouted very loudly:

"Why, my dear girl, it's appallingly late!"

Then everyone simultaneously took his watch from his pocket and exclaimed:—"How late it is!"

Only Lucian insinuated, out of politeness: "Last Friday it was later still!" But no one paid any attention to his remark (I said to him simply: "Your watch must be slow"); they all ran off to look for their overcoats; Angela was shaking people's hands, still smiling, and offering the last of the buns. And then she leaned over the banisters to see everyone down.—I waited for her, collapsed on a hassock. When she returned:

"Your at home has been a real nightmare!"—I began. "Oh! these men of letters! these men of letters, Angela!!! Unbearable, every one of them!!!"

"But that isn't what you were saying the other day," she replied.

"That, Angela, was because I hadn't seen them here with you.—And besides, it's frightening how many there were of them!—My dear, it simply isn't done to have as many as that at one time!"

"But," said she, "I hadn't invited them all; what happened was, that each one brought several more with him."

"In the middle of them all you looked so flustered. . . . You ought to have asked Laura to come up; you would have helped each other to keep in countenance."

"But," she replied, "it was because I saw you were so excited; I thought you were going to bite the furniture."

"Dear Angela, it was because otherwise everyone would have been so bored. . . . But how suffocating it was in your drawing-room!—Next time no one must be allowed in without an invitation-card.—And what, I ask you, was the meaning of your little ventilator! In the first place, nothing annoys me like things that turn round and round in the same place; you ought to know that by now!—And then, what a revolting noise it makes as it turns! One could hear it from under the curtain the moment one stopped talking. And everybody asked himself: "What can it be?"—You can imagine that I couldn't very well tell them: "It's Angela's ventilator!"—There, can you hear it now, squeaking away. Oh! it's unbearable, my dear, stop it, I entreat you."

"But," said Angela, "there's no way of stopping it."

"Ah! it too," I exclaimed; "—then let's talk very loudly, my dear.—Why! are you crying?"

"Not at all," said she, looking very flushed.

"A pity!"—And I declaimed, seized with a lyric impulse in order to drown that tiny cacophony:— "Angela! Angela! the time has come! Let us away from these intolerable purlieus!—Shall we suddenly hear, fair lady, the great sea-wind on the shores?—I realize that in in your presence one has only little thoughts, but that wind sometimes uplifts them. . . . Goodbye! I need to walk; only to-morrow, think of it! then the journey. But think of it, dear Angela, think of it!"

"Well, goodbye," said she; "go home and sleep. Goodbye."

I left her. I returned home almost at a run; I undressed; I lay down; not to sleep; when I see other people taking coffee, it makes me restless. And I felt distressed, and said to myself: "Did I really do all I could to persuade them? I ought to have found some more powerful arguments for Martin. . . . And Gustave!—Ah! so Valentine only likes madmen!—fancy calling me "sensible"!— how can he! I who've done nothing all day that wasn't absurd. I quite realize that isn't the same thing. . . . And here, my thought, why dost thou stop short and fix me with haggard, owl-like gaze?—Revolutionary? After all, perhaps that's what I am, from sheer horror of the contrary. How wretched one feels, for having wanted to stop being wretched!—To be unable to make oneself understood. . . . And yet, what I said to them was true—since it makes me suffer.—Does it make me suffer?—Oh dear! there are moments when I cease to understand in the least either what I want, or whom I blame for it; at such times it seems that I am struggling with phantoms of my own creation and that I . . . Oh God! God, truly that's a thing that weighs on one, and other people's thoughts are still more inert than matter. It's as if each idea, as soon as we touch upon it, wreaks its vengeance; ideas are like night-walking ghouls, that settle on your shoulders, feed upon you, and weigh the heavier the weaker they have made you . . . Now that I have begun to look for the equivalents of thoughts, in order to make them clearer to others—I can't stop; retrospections;—how ridiculous

61

these metaphors are;—I feel myself being gradually invaded, while I portray them, by all the maladies with which I reproach others, and I keep for myself all the suffering that I cannot succeed in giving to them. It seems to me now that the sensation I have of that suffering augments my malady still further, and that the others, perhaps, are not sick after all.—But then, they are right not to suffer—and I'm wrong to reproach them with not suffering;—yet I live as they do, and it's living so that makes me suffer . . . Ah! my head's in despair!—I want to disquiet people—I give myself a great deal of trouble to that end—and I disquiet no one but myself . . . Hullo! a phrase! let's make a note of it." I took out a sheet of paper from under my pillow, lit my candle again, and wrote these simple words:

"Become enamoured of one's own disquiet."

I blew out my candle.

". . . Oh God, God! before I go to sleep, there's one small point I'd like to examine further . . . One takes hold of a little idea—one would have done as well to leave it in peace . . . —Hey! . . . What? . . . Nothing, it's I who am speaking;—I was saying that one would have done as well to leave it in peace . . . Hey! . . . What? . . . Ah! I was going off to sleep . . . —no, I wanted to go on thinking about this little idea, which is growing larger; I don't altogether follow its development;— now the idea is enormous—and it has taken hold of me— in order to live upon me; yes, I am its means of existence; —it is ponderous—I have to present it, to represent it, in society.—It has seized upon me, so that I may trapse it around in society.—It is as heavy as God Himself. . . . Curse it! yet another phrase."—I took out another sheet of paper; I lit my candle and wrote:

"It must increase, but I must decrease."

"That's in St. John. . . . Ah! while I'm about it:"—I took out a third sheet . . .

.   .   .   .

"Now I can't remember what I was going to say . . . oh well! it can't be helped; I have a pain in the head . . . No, the thought would be lost,—lost . . . and I'd have a pain in its place, as in a wooden leg . . . wooden leg . . . the thought has gone, yet one can feel it . . . the thought . . . the thought . . . —when you repeat your words, it's because you're falling asleep; I shall repeat again: wooden leg . . . wooden l— . . . Ah! I haven't blown my candle out. . . . Yes, I have. . . . Have I blown my candle out? . . . Yes, since I'm asleep.—All the same, when Hubert came in again, it was still alight; . . . but Angela was positive that I had; . . . in fact, that was when I spoke to her about the wooden leg;—because it was getting stuck in the bog; I pointed out to her that I should never be able to run fast enough; this surface, I said, is horribly elastic! . . . it's the Dead Marsh in Saul—no, that's not right! . . . Hullo, where's Angela? I'm beginning to run a little faster.—Bother! it's frightful how one sinks in . . . I shall never be able to run fast enough . . . where is the boat? Have I reached it? . . . I'm going to jump—oof! hup!—Tiver my shimbers! . . .

"If you like, then, Angela, we will take a little pleasure-voyage in this shallop. I was simply pointing out, dear lady, that there is nothing there but carex and lycopodia —and lesser potamogetons—and I have nothing in my pockets—just the least morsel of breadcrumbs for the fish . . . Hullo! where's Angela? Really, dear lady, why are you all in a jelly this evening? . . . but you're dissolving completely, my dear!—Angela! Angela! do you hear— come now, do you hear? Angela! . . . and will no more of you remain than this stem of botanical waterlily (and I employ the word in a sense that is very difficult to appreciate nowadays)—which I am about to gather in the stream . . . But it's absolute velvet! a perfect carpet;— it's an elastic rug! . . . Then why stay sitting on it? with those two chair-legs in your hands. One really must try to come out from under the furniture!—We're expecting His Grace . . . all the more when it's so stifling here! . . . So here's the portrait of Hubert. How blooming he looks! . . . Let's open the door; it's too hot. This other room seems to me rather more as I expected to find it;— only the portrait of Hubert here isn't a very good one; I preferred the other; he looks like a ventilator; yes, indeed! the spit and image of a ventilator. Why is he giggling? . . . Let's go. Come, dear lady . . . hullo! where's Angela?—I had her very tightly by the hand just now; she must have slipped into the corridor, to go and pack her suit-case. She might at least have left the railway time-table . . . but don't run so fast, I shall never be able to keep up with you.—Ah! bother! another closed door. . . . Fortunately, they are very easy to open; I slam them behind me so that His Grace can't catch me.—I think he's put all Angela's drawing-room on my track. . . . What a crowd! what a lot of men of letters! . . . Bang!— Oh! shall we never get out of this corridor! Bang! these rooms are bang on top of each other! I don't know where I'm getting to. . . . How quickly I am running now! . . . Misery me! there aren't any more doors at all here. The portrait of Hubert is hung crooked;—it's going to fall;—he looks like a giggulator. . . . This room is much too strait and narrow—I shall even use the word: *exiguous*; we shall never be able to get everybody in. They're nearly here. . . . I'm suffocating!—Ah! through the window.—I am going to shut it behind me;—I am going to flutter dejectedly on to the balcony overlooking the street.—Hullo! it's a corridor! Ah! here they come:—Oh God, God! I'm going mad. . . . I'm suffocating!"

I awoke, soaked in sweat; the bedclothes were tucked in too tightly, and bound me in like bandages; their tension seemed like a horrible weight on my chest; I made a great effort, raised them, and with one jerk flung them all off. The air of my room was about me; I breathed methodically.—Coolness—first dawn—pale window-panes. . . . I shall have to take notes of all that;—aquarium, —it melts into the background of the room . . . At that moment I shivered;—I'm going to catch cold, I thought, —certainly, I'm catching cold.—And with chattering teeth, I rose to recover the bedclothes, and spreading them over the bed once more I submissively tucked myself in again for sleep.

HUBERT

OR

THE DUCKSHOOT

Friday.

As soon as I got out of bed I saw on the agenda: 'Try to get up at six.' It was eight o'clock; I took my pen; I crossed it out; I wrote in its place: 'Get up at eleven.'—And I went to bed again, without reading the rest.

After my horrible night I felt unwell, and instead of milk I took, by way of variety, a little barley-water; and I even went so far as to have it in bed, where my manservant brought it to me. As my agenda exasperated me, it was on a genuinely loose leaf that I wrote: 'This evening, buy a magnum of Évian water'—then I pinned this leaf on the wall.

"—In order to taste this water, I'll stay at home, I won't go to dine with Angela; besides, Hubert is going there; perhaps I'd be in their way;—but I'll go immediately afterwards in the evening, to see if I should have been in their way."

I took my pen and wrote: 'My dear, I have a sick headache; I shall not come to supper; besides, Hubert will be coming, and I shouldn't like to be in the way; but I'll come round immediately after in the evening.—I've had

66

a rather peculiar nightmare, about which I will tell you.'

I put the letter in an envelope; took another sheet, and quite calmly wrote:

"Tityrus goes by the pond-sides to gather useful plants. He finds some borage, efficacious marsh-mallow and extremely bitter centaury. He comes back with a bunch of simples. Because of the virtue of his plants, he looks for people to heal. Round the ponds, not a soul. He thinks: that's a pity.—Then he goes to the saltpans, where there are fevers and workmen. He goes up to them, talks to them, exhorts them, and gives them proof of their sickness;—but one says he is not sick, another, to whom Tityrus gives a medicinal flower, plants it in a vase and goes to watch it growing; yet another does indeed realize that he has fever, but believes it is good for his health.

And as in the end no one wishes to get well, and as this would have meant letting the flowers fade, Tityrus himself catches fever, so that he can at least give medical attention to himself."

At ten o'clock the bell rang; it was Alcides. He said: "In bed!—Are you ill?"

I said:—"No. Good morning, my dear fellow.—Nevertheless, I can't get up till eleven.—It's a resolution I have made.—What did you want?"

"To wish you goodbye; they told me you were off on a journey. . . . Are you to be away for long?"

"Not for very, very long. . . . You understand that with the limited means at my disposal . . . But the important thing is to leave.—Eh? I don't say that to get rid of you;—but I have a great deal to write before I . . . well, it was very nice of you to come;—*au revoir*." He left.

I took a new sheet and wrote:

"Tityre semper recubans"

and then I went to sleep again, and slept till noon.

67

It's a curious thing, and worth noting, how an important resolution, the decision to make a great change in one's life, makes all the petty obligations of the day, the common tasks, seem futile, and therefore gives one the strength to send them to the devil.

It was thanks to this that I had the courage to treat Alcides, whose visit disturbed me, with an incivility which otherwise I should never have dared.—Similarly, having chanced to see on the agenda, which I couldn't help glancing at, the following memorandum: 'Ten o'clock. Go and explain to Maglor why I think him so stupid,'—I had the strength to rejoice at my not having gone.

—'There's some good in the agenda,' I thought, 'for if I hadn't noted for this morning what I ought to have done, I might have forgotten it, and then I wouldn't have been able to rejoice at not having done it. Therein lies the constant charm for me of what I so neatly called the *negative unforeseen*; I'm partial to it, because it requires little organization, and therefore does very well for everyday use.'

In the evening, then, after dinner, I kept my appointment with Angela. She was seated at the piano; she was in the act of joining Hubert in singing the big duet from *Lohengrin*, which I was happy to interrupt.

—"Angela, my dear," said I on entering, "I haven't brought a suit-case; however I shall stay the night here, since you have so graciously invited me, and await with you, shall I not, the hour of our early-morning departure.—I believe I left here some time ago various objects which you will have put in my room: hobnailed boots, pullover, belt, sou'wester . . . We shall find all that I need. I'm not going back home again:—This last evening we must use all our ingenuity, think of to-morrow's departure, do nothing that does not serve as a preparation; we have to motivate it, lead up to it, render it in every respect desirable. Hubert must egg us on, by relating to us some past adventure."

"I haven't the time," said Hubert, "it's already late, and I have to go to my insurance society to see to some papers before the office closes.—Besides, I'm no good at telling stories, and the only ones I know are memories of my shooting expeditions.—This one goes back to my big journey in Judea;—but it is a terrible story, Angela, and I don't know . . ."

"Oh! tell it us, please do."

"Since you wish it,—here's the story:

"I was travelling with Bolbos,—whom neither of you can have known; he was a great friend of my childhood;—it's no use racking your brains, Angela, he's dead,—and it is his end that I am about to relate to you.

"He was, like myself, a great hunter, a hunter of tigers in the jungle. Moreover, he was vain, and he'd had made for him, out of the skin of one of the tigers he had himself killed, a fur-lined coat, in very bad taste, which he wore even on hot days, always wide open.—He was even wearing it on this last evening . . . with better reason, too, for it was almost too dark to see, and the cold was already keen, and growing keener. You know that in those climates the nights are very cold, and it's during the night that one hunts the panther. One hunts them on swings—and really, it's quite good fun. In the mountains of Idumea there are rocky defiles known to hunters, through which, at its usual hours, the beast passes; nothing is more regular in its habits than a panther—in fact that's what makes it possible to hunt them.—A panther has to be killed from above,—for anatomical reasons. Hence the use of the swing, though it only really offers all its advantages when one misses the panther. In fact, the recoil of the explosion causes an impulse strong enough to set the swing in motion; for this purpose one chooses a very light model; it starts off swinging at once, backwards and forwards, and the exasperated panther springs, but can't catch it—which it certainly would do, if one remained motionless. Would, did I say? . . . which it did! Which it did, Angela!

". . . These swings are suspended from one side of the ravine to the other; well, we had one each; it was late; we waited. The panther was due to pass beneath us between midnight and one o'clock. I was young then, a bit of a coward, and at the same time rash—I mean, hasty. Bolbos was older and wiser; experienced in this form of chase, my friend, as was his generous way, had yielded me the better place, whence I'd be first to glimpse our prey."

"When you make verses, they are completely worthless," I said to him; "so do try to speak in prose."

He resumed, without seeing what I meant.

"At midnight, I loaded my rifle. At a quarter past, the full moon rose over the rocks."

"What a beautiful sight that must have been!" said Angela.

"Soon one could hear, not far off, the faint, unmistakable rustling that the great felines make as they walk. Half an hour after midnight I saw a long, creeping shape advancing—it was the panther! I continued to wait, until it was directly below me.—I fired. . . . My dear Angela, how shall I express it? I felt myself and my swing suddenly impelled backwards,—I seemed to be flying through the air; in a flash, I was out of reach—I'd lost my head, but not enough to . . . But Bolbos hadn't fired!—What was he waiting for? I simply couldn't understand it;—but what I did understand was, that it's

very imprudent to go panther-hunting in couples:
suppose, you see, my dear Angela, that one of you fires
so much as a split second after the other;—the incensed
panther sees the motionless shape—has time to spring—
and yet, the one it catches is precisely the one who hasn't
fired.—I believe, when I think about it now, that Bolbos
meant to fire, but his gun wouldn't go off. Such mishaps
do occur, even with the best rifles. When I ceased my
backward motion and began to return forwards, I beheld
Bolbos with the panther on top of him, and both of them
on his swing, which by now was in violent movement;
in fact, nothing is more agile than these animals.

"Such, my dear Angela,—think of it! such was the
spectacle at which I was condemned to be a mere onlooker—I came and went, backwards and forwards I
swung;—and now Bolbos was swinging too, underneath
the panther—and I could do nothing about it!—Use my
rifle? Impossible: how could I aim?—I would have liked
at least to go away, for the swinging made me feel
horribly sick. . . ."

"How very moving that must have been," said
Angela.

"And now, goodbye, dear friends,—I must leave you.
I'm in a hurry. Have a good journey; enjoy yourselves;
don't be too late getting back.—I'll come and see you
again on Sunday."

Hubert left.

There was an enormous silence. If I had spoken, I
would have said: "Hubert told that very badly. I didn't
know about his journey in Judea. Was his story true?
While he was talking you looked as if you had a most
exaggerated admiration for him."—But I said nothing.
I looked at the hearth, the flame of the lamp, Angela
beside me, both of us beside the fire—the table—the

exquisite half-light of the room—all the things we were going to have to leave. Tea was brought in. It was past eleven o'clock; each of us seemed to be dozing off.

When midnight had ceased striking:

"I, too, have hunted," I began.

Amazement appeared to wake her; she said:

"You! Hunted! Hunted what?"

"Duck, Angela. And what's more, with Hubert; it was long ago. . . . But, my dear Angela, whyever not?—What I dislike is not hunting, but guns; I do hate explosions. You are mistaken, I assure you, in your judgment of me. I have a very active temperament; it's the apparatus that I dislike . . . But Hubert, always well-informed about the latest inventions, had procured me for the winter, through the good offices of Amadeus, a compressed-air rifle."

"Oh tell me all!" said Angela.

"It was not," I continued, "—it was not, you may well imagine, one of those extraordinary rifles such as one sees only at big exhibitions;—besides, I had only hired it, for these instruments are horribly expensive; and then, I don't like to keep firearms in the house.—A small air-chamber operated the trigger,—by means of an elastic tube passed beneath the armpit; one held in the hand a rather 'tired' bulb,—for the instrument was an old one;—at the least pressure the rubber bulb fired the bullet. . . . Your ignorance of ballistics prevents me from explaining more clearly."

"You ought to have shown it to me," said Angela.

"My dear, these weapons can only be touched by quite specially skilled hands,—and then, as I've already told you, I didn't keep it. Besides, this single night's hunting sufficed, it was so fructiferous, to wear out the bulb once and for all,—as I am about to relate to you:—It was a misty night in December.—Hubert said to me: 'Are you coming?" I answered him: "I am ready."

"He unhooked his fowling-piece from its peg, and I my rifle; he took his bird-calls and his boots; we took our nickel-plated skates. Then, with that instinct peculiar to hunters, we advanced through the darkness. Hubert knew the path leading to the hut where, near the game-frequented pond, a peat fire, damped under its ashes, had been ready for us since dusk. Besides, as soon as we left the park, which was overgrown with gloomy firtrees, the night seemed almost clear. A moon, swollen nearly to full-ness, showed indistinctly, through the ethereal mist. It was not as one sometimes sees it, visible by fits and starts, now hidden, now streaming over the clouds; the night was not restless;—nor, on the contrary, was it a peaceful night;—it was mute, idle, moist and, would you have understood me if I had said: passionless. The sky was all of a piece; you could have turned it over without surprise.—If I insist so, calm friend, it is to make you fully understand the degree to which that night was ordinary.

"Experienced sportsmen know that these are the best nights to lie in wait for duck. We reached the channel, whose frozen water we could distinguish, through the withered reeds, by its polished reflection. We put on our skates and, without speaking a word, glided on. The nearer we approached to the pond, the more the muddy water, shallowing, mixed with mosses and earth and half-melted snow, made our progress difficult. The chan-nel gradually disappeared; in the end our skates hampered us. We walked. Hubert entered the hut to get warm; as for myself, I couldn't stay there, because the smoke was so dense . . . What I am about to tell you, Angela, is a terrible thing!—for listen!—As soon as Hubert had

warmed himself, he entered the oozy water; I know very
well he had his waterproof boots and oilskin. clothing—
but, my dear, he didn't go in up to the knees—nor up
to the waist: he went in over his head!—Do not shudder
more than you need; he did it on purpose! In order to
hide himself better from the ducks, he wanted to dis-
appear completely; it was mean, you are about to say . . .
Yes, wasn't it? I felt so too; but that is why the game
came in abundance. We took our positions; I sat in the
bottom of a moored punt, and waited for the flight to
draw near.—Hubert, when he was well hidden, began to
call the duck. For this purpose he used two bird-calls:
one for the call, the other for the reply. The distant flight
heard him; then it heard the reply; duck are so stupid,
that they thought this was their own voice; so they
hurried up—to be in time to have uttered it, dear Angela.
—Hubert's imitation was perfect. The sky above us grew
dark with their triangular cloud; then the noise of their
wings increased, because then they came down; and when
they were close enough, I began to fire.

"Soon they came in such numbers that, to tell the truth,
I scarcely took the trouble to aim; I contented myself with
pressing the bulb a little harder each time I fired,—so
easily did the trigger work; the only noise it made was
that of a roman candle at the moment it goes off—or
rather, the sound of *"Palm!"* in a line of Monsieur
Mallarmé. Often, indeed, one couldn't hear it at all, and
when I didn't put my ear close to the barrel, I could
only tell that the bullet had left the gun, by the fall of
another bird. For a long time, hearing no sound, the
ducks lingered. They fell, turning on the brown water
encrusted with miry scum, and in their contortions tore
off leaves with the wings they struggled in vain to close.
They tried, before dying, to find shelter in bushes, as the

reeds did not hide them. A few feathers loitered behind, floating on the water, in the air, and seeming light as the mists. . . . I began to ask myself: When will it end?— Finally, as day started to break, the last survivors flew away; suddenly there was a great noise of wings, whose meaning the dying remnant understood.—Then at last Hubert reappeared, covered with leaves and ooze. We unmoored the punt, and pushing it with poles through the bruised reed-stems, in the hideous light that precedes dawn, we gathered up our victuals.—I had killed more than forty;—all of them smelled of mud. . . . But why! are you asleep, dear Angela?"

The lamp burned low from lack of oil; the fire was dying joylessly, and the windowpane was bathed in dawn. A morsel of hope seemed at long last to descend, with chattering teeth, from the granaries of heaven. . . . Ah! may there come to us at last a drop of celestial dew, and in this room so narrow, where we slumbered so long, may a dawn, even behind the windowpane, even rainy, at length appear, and may it bring even unto us, through the accumulated shadow, a gleam of natural daylight. . . .

Angela was half-asleep; not hearing the sound of my voice, she awoke gently—murmured:

"You ought to put that into . . ."

". . . Ah! for pity's sake do not finish your sentence, my dear—and don't tell me I ought to put that into *Marshlands*.—For one thing, it is there already—and then, you haven't been listening—but I don't blame you!—no, I entreat you, do not think that I blame you. Besides, I want to be full of joy to-day. Day is dawning, Angela! see! See the grey roofs of the town, and those patches of white on the suburbs. . . . Will it be . . . Ah! from what dismal greyness, and from what exhausted vigil,—the bitter ash, ah! of thought—will it be thy white candour,

75

gliding unhoped for, dawn, that will deliver us?—The casement where the morning streams . . . no . . . the morning where the casement pales. . . . Angela—would wash . . . would wash . . .

> '*We will depart! I feel that somewhere birds*
> *Are drunk with joy!*'

Angela! that is a line of Monsieur Mallarmé's!—I quote it rather inaccurately—the original is in the singular—but you are departing too—ah! my dear, I'm taking you away with me!—Suit-cases!—let us hasten;—I want my haversack to be crammed to the brim!—However, we mustn't take too many things: "Everything that one can't pack into one's suit-case is unbearable!"—That is a saying of Monsieur Barrès—Barrès, you know, he's a member of the Chamber of Deputies, my dear!—Ah! it's stifling here; if you don't mind, let's open the window! I am extremely agitated. Quick, go to the kitchen. When travelling one never knows where one will get dinner. Let us take four stuffed rolls, some eggs, some sausage and the loin of veal left over from supper yesterday."

Angela withdrew; I remained alone for a moment.

Now, of that moment what should I say?—Why not speak of it, just as much as of the instant that followed: do we know which are the really important things? What arrogance there is in *choice*!—Let us look upon everything with equal insistence, and before the agitation of departure, may I yet have a calm interlude of meditation. Let us look! Let us look!—What do I see?

—Three vegetable-hawkers passing.

—An omnibus, already.

—A doorkeeper sweeping in front of his door.

—Shopkeepers cleaning their shopwindows.

—The cook going to market.

—Schoolboys on their way to school.

—Newspapers being delivered at kiosks. Gentlemen in a hurry buying them.

—Tables being put out at a café.

Oh God! God, let not Angela come in just now; here I am sobbing again . . . It's nerves, I think;—it takes me like that whenever I make lists of things.—Besides, now my teeth are chattering. For the love of me, let's shut that window. This morning air has chilled me to the bone. Life—other people's life!—is that life? Seeing life! To think that that is living! ! . . . And what else could one say about it? Exclamations.—Now I'm sneezing; yes, as soon as thought stops and contemplation begins, I catch cold.—But I hear Angela—let us hasten.

ANGELA

OR

THE LITTLE JOURNEY

Saturday.

ONLY TAKE NOTES on the poetic moments of the journey—because they are more in keeping with what I meant it to be.

In the cab that took us to the station, I declaimed:

> *"Goats beside the torrents graze,*
> *Bridges across the gorges march,*
> *The larch its serried ranks arrays . . .*
> *Whence climbs with us (or am I wrong?)*
> *The resinous scent, delicious, strong,*
> *Of the firtree, of the larch."*

"Oh!" said Angela, "—What a beautiful poem!"

"Do you think so, my dear," said I. "—But no, it isn't, I assure you; I don't say it's bad, exactly. . . . But still, I don't set great store by it;—I was just improvising. —And then, perhaps you are right;—it may be good after all. The author himself can never really tell. . . ."

We arrived at the station much too early. There was, in the waiting-room, ah! a really long wait. It was then,

while I was sitting beside Angela, that I felt it my duty
to say something kind to her:

"My friend—my dear friend,"—I began; "in your
smile there is a sweetness which I can scarcely understand. Could it come from your sensibility?"

"I don't know," she replied.

"Sweet Angela! I had never appreciated you so well as
I do to-day."

I also said to her: "Charming friend, what delicacy you
show in your trains of thought!" and something else that
I can't remember.

A road bordered with aristolochia.

About three o'clock—without so much as a by your
leave, a little shower began to fall.

"It won't be more than a spot," said Angela.

"Why," I said to her, "—my dear, when the weather
is so unsettled, why only bring a sunshade?"

"It's an all-weathers model," said she.

However, as it was raining harder, and I'm always
afraid of damp, we went back to shelter under the roof
of the cider-press shed that we had just left.

From the tops of the pine-trees, slowly descending,
one by one, in a brown single file, one could see the
processional caterpillars—which, at the foot of the pine-
trees, long awaited, the fat ground-beetles gobbled up.

"I didn't see the ground-beetles!" said Angela (for I
showed her this sentence).

"Nor I, dear Angela,—nor the caterpillars either.—
Besides, it's the wrong time of year; but this sentence,
don't you agree, is an excellent rendering of the impression made by our journey. . . .

"It is just as well, after all, that this little journey has been a failure—since as it is it will be more instructive to you."

"Oh! why do you say that?" replied Angela.

"But, my dear—please understand that the pleasure a journey may procure us is a mere accessory. One travels for the sake of education. . . . Why!—Are you crying, my dear?"

"Certainly not!" said she.

"Well! A pity.—Still, you are flushed."

SUNDAY

O^{N THE AGENDA:}
10 o'clock: church.

Visit Richard.

About five o'clock go with Hubert to visit the poverty-stricken Rosselange family and Grabu, the little gardener.

Find an opportunity of pointing out to Angela how serious my jokes are.

Finish *Marshlands*.—Gravity.

It was nine o'clock. I felt the solemnity of this day from the recrudescence of my agony. I propped my head gently upon my hand; I wrote:

'All through life I shall have struggled towards a little greater light. I have seen, ah! all round me, crowds of beings languishing in too narrow rooms; the sun never entered them; great panes of tinted glass brought them, about midday, discoloured refractions of its light. It was the hour when, in the alleys below, one stifled in the breathless heat; rays, that could find no space to diffuse themselves, concentrated between the walls of the houses an unhealthy shimmering. Those who had seen them thought of open spaces, of rays lighting on the foam of breaking waves and on the corn that grows on the plains. . . .'

81

Angela came in:

I cried: "You! my dear Angela."

She said: "Are you working? You are sad this morning.
I felt it. I have come."

"Dear Angela! . . . But—do sit down.—Why should I
be sadder this morning?"

"Oh! you are sad, aren't you? And it wasn't true, what
you were saying yesterday . . . You can't be glad that
our journey wasn't quite as we had hoped."

"Sweet Angela! . . . I am genuinely touched by your
words . . . Yes, I am sad, my dear;—my soul this morning really is very dejected."

"I have come to console it," said she.

"How we do relapse, my dear! Everything is much
sadder now.—I had counted a good deal, I confess, on
this journey, I believed it would give a new direction to
my talent. It was you who proposed it to me, it's true,
but I had been thinking of it for many years. I am better
aware now of all I would have liked to leave behind,
from seeing all that is restored to me on my return."

"Perhaps," said Angela, "we didn't go far enough
away.—But it would have taken two days to see the
sea and we wanted to be back on Sunday in time for
church."

"We had not given enough thought, Angela, to that
coincidence;—and besides, how far ought we to have
gone? How we do relapse, dear Angela!—When one
thinks back on it, now it is over: how very sad was our
journey!—The word 'aristolochia' expresses something
of the kind.—You will remember for many a day that
little meal in the damp shed with the cider-press, and how,
afterwards, we said nothing, and shivered. Stay with me
—stay here all the morning, ah! I beg of you.—I feel I
am going to burst into tears in a moment. It seems that

I carry *Marshlands* always with me—*Marshlands* will never bore anyone so much as it has bored me. . . ."

"Supposing you gave it up," she said.

"Angela! Angela, you don't understand! I give it up here; I find it again there; I find it again everywhere; the sight of other people obsesses me with it, and this little journey will not have delivered me from it.—We don't wear out our melancholy, in re-making every day our yesterdays we don't wear out our maladies, we wear out nothing but ourselves, and every day we lose some of our energy.—What prolongations of the past!—I fear death, dear Angela.—Shall we never be able to put anything outside time—and not be obliged to re-make it? —Some work at long last which will no longer have need of us in order to endure?—But of all that we do, nothing endures the moment we cease to keep it going. And yet all our actions subsist horribly and weigh upon us. What weighs on us is the necessity of repeating them; there's something there that I no longer quite understand. —Excuse me—just a second. . . ."

And taking a sheet of paper I wrote: '*We have to maintain our actions when they are not sincere.*'

I resumed: "But do you understand, dear Angela, that this is what made our journey a failure. . . . There's nothing we can leave behind and say: "THAT EXISTS." So that we came back in order to see whether everything was still there.—Ah! mercy on us, shall we, then, never have made others do anything! nothing! except to tow this drifting flotsam back to port . . . And our relationship, dear Angela! could anything be more transitory! In fact that is the very thing, you understand, which enables us to go on with it for so long."

"Oh! you are unfair," said she.

"No, my dear—no, it's not that,—but I am anxious

to make you realize the impression of sterility that emanates from it."

Then Angela bowed her head, and smiling faintly, out of decorum:

"This evening, I'll stay with you," said she; "—would you like me to?"

I exclaimed: "Oh! really, my dear!—If one can't talk to you any more about such things, without your immediately . . . —Besides, you must admit you don't very much want to;—and then, you are, I assure you, delicate, and I was thinking of you when I wrote, do you remember, the following sentence: '*She feared pleasure as a thing that was too violent and might perhaps have killed her.*' You declared it was exaggerated. No, my dear,—no—and it might be an embarrassment to us; I've even composed some verses on the subject:

. . . .

> '*We are not, I suppose,*
> *Dear lady, among those*
> *Of whom the sons of men derive their birth.*'

(The rest of the poem is very moving, but too long to quote now.)—Besides, I'm not very strong myself, as I have tried to express in the following lines, which you won't easily forget now:—(they are the least bit exaggerated.)

> '. . . *But thou, of all men frailest here below,*
> *What can'st thou, or what would'st thou, do?*
> *Is it thy passion, say,*
> *Will give thee strength at last,*
> *Or here at home to stay,*
> *And lull thyself to rest?*'

And you can easily see from that, that I really did want to go out. . . . It's true that I added, in a manner which is still sadder, I might even say discouraged:

> 'If thou go'st, ah! beware of—what?
> If thou remain'st, yet worse the ill.
> Death follows close, be certain that
> He'll take thee, say no word, and kill.'

. . . The rest is about you and isn't finished.—But if you want it very much. . . . Invite Barnaby instead!"

"Oh! How cruel you are this morning," said Angela;— she added: "He doesn't smell nice."

"But precisely, dear Angela; strong men never smell nice.—That is what my young friend Tancred has tried to express in the following line:

> *Victorious captains smell abominably!*

(I know what astonishes you: it's the scansion.)—But how flushed you are! . . . And then, I only meant to make you realize.—Ah! I also wanted, my delicate friend, to find an opportunity of pointing out to you how serious my jokes are. . . . Angela! I am terribly tired! . . . I shall burst into tears quite soon. . . . But first, let me dictate a few sentences to you; you write faster than I do; besides, I can walk up and down while I'm speaking; I find it helps. Here is a pencil and paper. Ah! sweet friend! what a good thing you came! Write, write as quickly as you can; besides, it's about our poor little journey:

. . . "There are some people who are out of doors in a moment. Nature knocks at their door: it opens on the vast plain in which, as soon as they emerge, their dwelling is forgotten and lost to sight. They find it again in the evening, when they need it to sleep in; they find it again easily. They might, if they wished, sleep beneath the stars, leave their house for a whole day,—forget it, even, for a long time.—If you find that natural, it's because you don't understand what I mean. You ought to be more astonished at these things . . . I assure you that, as for ourselves, if we envy these dwellers in freedom, it's because, every time we have built in toil and sorrow some roof to shelter us, this roof has followed us, has set itself from that day forth over our heads; has sheltered us from rain, it's true, but has hidden the sun from us. We have slept in its shadow; we have worked, danced, made love, meditated in its shadow;—sometimes, so great was the splendour of the dawn, we have thought we might escape one morning; we have tried to forget it; we have crept like thieves under the thatch, not to break in, not we, but to break out—surreptitiously—and we have run towards the plain. And the roof ran after us. It bounded along like the bell in the legends after the people who tried to miss church. We never ceased to feel its weight on our heads. Already, in order to construct it, we had carried all its materials; now we gauged the weight of the whole. It bent our heads, it bowed our shoulders,—as the weight of the Old Man of the Sea did to Sindbad.—At first one doesn't notice; then, it's terrible, it attaches itself to us solely by virtue of its weight. One can't get rid of it. Once we take up an idea, we must carry it to the very end.

"Ah!" said Angela, "hapless, hapless friend—why did you ever begin *Marshlands?*—when there are so many other subjects—and even more poetic ones."

"Precisely, Angela! Write! Write!—(Oh God! am I at last going to be able to be sincere to-day?)

"I don't at all understand what you mean by your more or less poetic. All the agonies of a consumptive cramped in his narrow room, of a miner longing to ascend once more into the light of day, of a pearl-diver feeling all the weight of the sea's dark waters pressing upon him! all the affliction of Plautus or Samson turning their mills, of Sisyphus rolling his stone; all the oppression of a nation reduced to slavery—all these pains, and many others, all these have I known."

"You dictate too fast," said Angela, "—I can't keep up with you."

"Then it can't be helped!—stop writing;—listen, Angela! Listen—for my soul is in despair. How many times, how many times have I made this gesture, as in some appalling nightmare, in which I imagined the canopy of my bed breaking loose, falling, enveloping me, pressing on my chest—and then, half sitting up, after I awoke—in order to push back, with outstretched arms, I know not what invisible walls—this gesture of repelling someone whose unwholeso ne breath I felt too near me— of holding back, with arms outstretched, walls that incessantly close in, or whose ponderous fragility rocks and totters over our heads; this gesture, also, of casting off too heavy clothing, too cumbersome cloaks, from over our shoulders. How many times, seeking a little fresh air, stifling, have I known the gesture of opening the windows—and I have stopped myself, void of hope, because once, when I did open them . . ."

"You caught cold?" said Angela.

". . . Because once, when I did open them, I saw they looked out only on backyards—or on other low-ceilinged rooms—on wretched backyards, sunless and airless—and then, beholding this, in my distress, I shouted with all my strength: "Lord! Lord! we are terribly shut in!"— and my voice returned to me as loud as it left my lips, from the low ceiling.—Angela! Angela! What shall we do now? Shall we try once more to lift these winding-sheets that oppress us—or shall we accustom ourselves to scarcely breathing—to prolonging, as we now do, our life in this tomb?"

"We have never been more alive," said Angela. "Could anyone, tell me truly, be more alive? What gave you the feeling of any greater exuberance? Who has told you that it was possible?—Was it Hubert?—Is he more alive because he is always bustling?"

"Angela! Angela! Look how I am sobbing now! Can it be that you have begun to understand my anguish? Can it be that I have at last put some bitterness into your smile?—Why! I declare! now you're crying.—Splendid! I'm happy! I'm in action!—I shall be able to finish *Marshlands*!"

Angela wept, and as she wept her long hair came loose and fell.

It was then that Hubert came in. Seeing us dishevelled: "Excuse me!—I'm disturbing you," he said, making as if to go away again.

This discretion touched me deeply; so much so that I cried:

"Come in! Come in, my dear Hubert! No one can ever disturb *us*!" and then I sadly added: "Isn't that so, Angela?"

She replied: "Yes, we were just having a talk."

"This is only a passing visit," said Hubert "—and I only want to say a few words. I am leaving for Biskra the day after to-morrow;—I've persuaded Roland to come with me."

I became suddenly indignant: "Presumptuous Hubert—it was I, I who persuaded him. We were just leaving Abel's together—I remember—when I told him he ought to make this journey."

Hubert burst out laughing; he said:

"You? but my poor friend, do please consider that you'd had enough of it when you'd gone as far as Montmorency! how can you pretend? . . . Anyway, it may well be that you were the first to speak to him about it; but tell me, please, what is the use of putting ideas into people's heads? Do you think that is what makes them act? And what's more, while we're on the subject, let me assure you that you are strangely lacking in propulsive force. . . . You can only give to others what you have yourself.—In short, do you want to come with us? . . .—no? Well then! what did I tell you? . . . So, dear Angela, goodbye—I'll see you again before I go."

He left.

"As you see, sanctimonious Angela,"—said I—"I am staying with you . . . but don't think it's out of love . . ."

"O no! I quite understand . . . " she replied.

". . . But, Angela, look!" I cried with a glimmering of hope: "it's nearly eleven! Oh! now it's too late for church!"

Then, with a sigh, she said:

"We'll go to the four o'clock service."

And everything was as bad as ever.

Angela had to go.

Happening to look at the agenda I noticed the memorandum about visiting the poor; I rushed to the post-office and sent a telegram:

"Oh! Hubert!—what about your charities! !"

Then I returned and reread *Little Lenten Lessons* while waiting for the answer.

At two o'clock his telegram came:—It read:

"Balls, letter follows."

Then dejection invaded me still more completely.

"For, if Hubert goes away," I groaned,—"who will come to see me at six o'clock?—When *Marshlands* is finished, God only knows what there will be left for me to do.—I know that neither poetry nor playwriting . . . I'm not good at them—and my aesthetic principles are opposed to my conceiving a novel.—I had thought of taking up my old subject of NETHERLANDS again—it would make a good sequel to *Marshlands*, and wouldn't make me contradict myself . . ."

At three o'clock an express-messenger brought me Hubert's letter; it read as follows: "—I leave my five indigent families in your care; a document will follow with a list of their names and all necessary information; as for my various other affairs, I'm entrusting them to Richard and his brother-in-law, for you would be quite incompetent to handle them. Goodbye—I'll write to you from over there."

Then I reopened my agenda and on Monday's leaf I wrote: "Try to get up at 6 o'clock."

. . . At half past three I went to call for Angela;—and we went together to the service at the Oratory.

At five o'clock—I went to see my poor people.— Then, as the day was growing cool, I returned home—I shut my windows and began writing . . .

At six o'clock, in came my great friend Jasper.

He was on his way from fencing-school. He said:

"I say! Are you working?"

I replied: "I am writing *Netherlands* . . ."

.   .   .   .

ENVOI

Oh! How the day has taken pains
Ever since dawn to wash the plains!

*We played you music on the flute
But you have not listened to it.*

*We have sung songs
You have not danced dances.*

*And when at last we deigned to dance
They had stopped playing the flute.*

*Therefore since our misfortune
I prefer the gentle moon.*

*She the despairing watch-dogs goads
And wakes to song harmonious toads.*

*In the deep well-meaning meres
Her silent widening face appears;*

*And her warm nudity
Bleeds to eternity.*

*Although we had no shepherd's crook,
The flocks to our sweet huts we took,*

*But the sheep asked for revelries
And scorned our useless prophecies.*

*So others lead, as if to water,
The white flocks to the place of slaughter.*

*And we have built upon the sand
Cathedrals too infirm to stand.*

ALTERNATIVE

Or shall I go yet once more, oh forest full of mystery—
to the place I know, where in a brown dead water the
leaves still soak and soften, the leaves of fallen years, of
lost delicious Aprils?

It is there that my broken resolutions take their
deepest rest, there that my thoughts are reduced, at long
last, to little or nothing.

THE END

LIST
OF
THE MOST REMARKABLE PHRASES
IN *MARSHLANDS*

* Wishing to respect personal idiosyncrasies, we leave to the individual reader the task of filling this page.

PROMETHEUS MISBOUND

An eagle, or a vulture, or a dove.
VICTOR HUGO.

CONTENTS

IN THE MONTH of May, 189. . ., at two o'clock in the afternoon, the following incident was seen to occur, and might well have been thought odd.

On the boulevard which leads from the Madeleine to the Opéra, a stout, middle-aged gentleman, whose unusual corpulence was his sole remarkable feature, was accosted by a thin gentleman, who smilingly, and, in our opinion, without ill intention, restored to the other a handkerchief which he had just let fall. The stout gentleman thanked him briefly and was about to continue his way, when, changing his mind, he leaned towards the thin person, and must have made some enquiry, which the latter must have answered; for the stout gentleman took a portable inkwell and a choice of pens from his pocket, and held them out unceremoniously to the thin gentleman, together with an envelope which till then he had held in his hand. And the passers-by could see the thin man promptly writing an address on the envelope.— But here begins the oddity of the story, which, nevertheless, was not reported in any of the newspapers: the thin gentleman, after giving back the pen and the envelope, had not had time to smile a goodbye, when the stout gentleman, by way of expressing his thanks, applied his hand abruptly to the other's cheek; he then jumped into a cab and disappeared, before any of the spectators who had gathered round (I was one of them), could recover from their surprise and think of stopping him.

I learned afterwards that it was Zeus, the banker.

The thin gentleman, visibly embarrassed by the interest which the public lavished upon him, declared he had scarcely felt the blow, although the blood was pouring from his nostrils and his cut lip. He begged that he might kindly be left alone, and, faced with his insistence, the passers-by at last withdrew. The reader will allow us, therefore, to pay no further attention for the present to a person of whom he will see quite enough in the sequel.

A CHRONICLE OF PRIVATE MORALITY

I

I SHALL SAY NOTHING about public morality, because there's no such thing. But while we're on the subject, here is an anecdote.

When, on the summit of the Caucasus, Prometheus had become fully aware that his chains, fetters, strait-waistcoats, prison-walls and other scruples, taking them all in all, were giving him pins and needles, in order to change his posture he rose on his left side, stretched out his right arm, and, between four and five o'clock on an autumn afternoon, walked down the boulevard which leads from the Madeleine to the Opéra.

Various Parisian celebrities passed—as many as one could possibly wish—before his eyes. 'Where are they going to?' Prometheus asked himself, and sitting down outside a café in front of a glass of beer, he enquired: "Waiter! Where are they going to?"

THE STORY OF THE WAITER AND THE MIGLIONAIRE

"If Monsieur saw them passing to and fro every day, as I do," said the waiter, "he might just as well ask where they come from. It must amount to much the same thing, since they pass backwards and forwards every day. I say to myself: if they pass to and fro, it's because they haven't found what they're looking for. I am now waiting for Monsieur to ask: What *are* they looking for?, because then Monsieur will see how I mean to answer him."

Then Prometheus asked:

"What *are* they looking for?"

The waiter replied:

"As they don't stay there, it can't be for happiness. Monsieur will believe me if he likes," and drawing nearer he said in a lower voice: "What they are looking for, is their personality. Monsieur is a stranger here?"

"Yes," said Prometheus.

"One can tell that at a glance," said the waiter. "Yes: their personality; or, as we call it here, their idiosyncrasy. Take me for an example: as you see me, you'd give your oath that I am a waiter. Well, now! Monsieur, you would be wrong; that's not my trade, but my hobby. You can believe me if you like: I have an inner life: I observe. There's nothing so interesting as personalities, and the relations between personalities. The restaurant here is very well arranged; the tables are all for three; I will explain how it's managed later on. You're going to have dinner soon, aren't you? We'll have you introduced."

Prometheus was rather tired. The waiter went on:

"Tables for three, yes, I've found that the most convenient system. Three gentlemen arrive; we introduce them (when they request it, naturally), because in my restaurant, before you can have dinner, you have to give your name; and then you have to say what you do; if you make a mistake, it can't be helped. Then you sit down (but I don't); you talk (there again, I don't)—but

106

I set relationships going; I listen, I scrutinize, I direct the conversation. When dinner is over I know three inner beings, three personalities! But they don't. As for me, you understand, I listen, I relate; they undergo the relationship. You will ask me: what does it bring in? Oh! nothing whatever. My private hobby is to create relationships. . . . Oh! not for my own benefit. . . . It's what you might call an absolutely gratuitous action."

Prometheus seemed rather tired. The waiter went on: "A gratuitous action! Does that mean nothing to you? To me it seems extraordinary. I have long thought that it is gratuitous action which distinguishes man from the animals. I used to call man, the animal capable of a gratuitous action. And then afterwards I thought the opposite—that man is the only creature that is incapable of acting gratuitously. Gratuitously! just imagine: without reason—yes, I know what you're thinking—let's say: without motive; he's incapable of it! And then it began to irritate me. I said to myself: why does he do this? Why does he do that? . . . That doesn't mean that I believe in determinism. . . . But, while we're on the subject, here is an anecdote:

"I have a friend, Monsieur, though you wouldn't believe it, who is a Miglionaire. He's intelligent, besides. He said to himself: a gratuitous action? how's it done? And you must understand that it doesn't mean an action that brings in no profit, for otherwise. . . . No, but a gratuitous act: one that isn't motivated by anything. Do you understand? Neither interest, passion, nor anything else. A disinterested act; self-born; an act without an end in view; and therefore without a master; a free act; an autochthonous Act!"

"Eh?" exclaimed Prometheus.

"Follow me carefully," said the waiter. "My friend

goes out, one fine morning, with a five-hundred-franc note in an envelope and a slap ready in his hand.

"The idea is to find someone without deliberately choosing him. So he lets his handkerchief drop in the street, and to the man who picks it up (a good-natured person, or he wouldn't have done so) the Miglionaire says:

"I beg your pardon, sir, but do you happen to know anyone?"

The other: "Yes, several people."

The Miglionaire: "In that case, sir, I presume you will be so kind as to write a name on this envelope; here is a choice of pens, a bottle of ink, a pencil. . . ."

The other writes, out of the goodness of his heart, and then says: "Now will you explain to me, sir . . .?"

The Miglionaire replies: "I'm doing this on principle"; and then (I forgot to tell you that he is very strong) he applies to the other's cheek the slap that he had ready in his hand, hails a cab, and disappears.

"Do you see? Two gratuitous actions at one swoop: a 500 franc note to an address he hasn't chosen, and a slap for someone who has chosen himself to pick up the handkerchief. Well! what could be more gratuitous than that? And as for the relationship! I don't mind betting you're not giving proper attention to the relationship. For, since the act is gratuitous, it's what we call here: reversible. One gets 500 francs for a slap in the face, the other a slap in the face for 500 francs . . . , and then it becomes too bewildering . . . one loses track.—Think of it! A gratuitous action! There's nothing more demoralizing.—But Monsieur is beginning to get hungry; I beg Monsieur's pardon; I've been letting myself run on. . . . If Monsieur would be so kind as to tell me his name,— so that I can introduce him. . . ."

"Prometheus," said Prometheus simply.

"Prometheus! Didn't I say Monsieur must be a stranger here . . . And what does Monsieur do?

"Nothing," said Prometheus.

"Oh! no. No," said the waiter with a gentle smile. "One has only to look at Monsieur, to see that he must have done something."

"It was such a long time ago," stammered Prometheus.

"Too bad, too bad," replied the waiter. "But Monsieur needn't worry; when I make the introductions, I give the names, of course, if the gentlemen wish it, but I never say what people do.—Come, come: Monsieur used to . . ."

"Make safety-matches," murmured Prometheus, blushing.

There was a rather painful silence; the waiter realized that he'd been wrong to insist, and Prometheus saw that he'd been wrong to reply. Then the waiter resumed, in a consoling voice:

"Oh well! Monsieur doesn't make them any more. But then, what? I really must put something down, I can't write plain 'Prometheus', just like that. Monsieur must have some little profession, a speciality . . . Well, now, what is Monsieur good at?"

"Nothing," said Prometheus again.

"Then let's put: man of letters. Now, if Monsieur will be so kind as to come inside; I can't serve people out here." And he shouted: "A table for three! One! . . ."

Two gentlemen came in, one through each door. They could be seen giving their names to the waiter; but as they did not ask to be introduced, they both sat down without more delay.

And when they were seated:

II

"Gentlemen," said one of them—"if I have come to this restaurant, seeing that the food here is very bad, it's entirely for the sake of the conversation. I hate having meals alone, and this system of tables for three suits me, for if they were for two one might start quarrelling. . . . But you seem very reserved?"

"I don't mean to," said Prometheus.

"Shall I go on?"

"Please do."

"Well, it's my belief that, during a meal lasting one hour, three people who have not met before have time to get acquainted;—they can do so by not eating too much (which is easy enough here); not talking much; and avoiding common ground, I mean, by saying nothing that is not strictly individual to themselves. I don't maintain that this conversation is indispensable, but if it affords us no pleasure, seeing that the food here is very bad, what are you doing in this restaurant?"

Prometheus was extremely tired; the waiter, leaning towards him, said in a whisper:

"That was Cocles. The one who is about to speak, is Damocles."

Damocles said:

THE STORY OF DAMOCLES

"Sir, if you had said that to me a month ago, I should have had precisely nothing to say in reply; but, after what happened to me last month, not a vestige of what I previously thought survives. I would refrain, therefore, from telling you my old ideas, were it not that some knowledge of them is needed to help you to understand in what respect my new ones differ from them. Well, gentlemen, for the past thirty days I have felt that I am a unique and original being, fitted with a truly singular destiny. From which, gentlemen, you may infer that before then I felt precisely the contrary. I led a perfectly ordinary life, and made a duty of this formula: to resemble the commonest of men. Now, of course, I realize that a common man cannot possibly exist, and I maintain that it is a vain ambition to try to resemble everybody, since everybody is the sum total of anybody, and anybody resembles nobody. No matter; I used all my ingenuity; I collected statistics, I worked out the golden mean, and never understood that extremes join hands, that the man who goes to bed very late meets the man who gets up very early, and he who chooses to take his seat on the golden mean, risks falling between two stools.

I used to go to bed every evening at ten o'clock. I slept for eight and a half hours. I took care in all my actions always to imitate the majority, and in all my thoughts to adopt the most usual opinion. I will refrain from insisting further on this point.

But now, what should happen to me one morning but a personal adventure. The importance of such an occurrence in the life of an orderly person can only be understood by its sequel. It's a precedent. It's horrible. It happened to me."

III

"Just imagine, then, that one morning I received a letter.—Gentlemen, I see, from the absence of your amazement, that I am telling my story badly. I ought to have said at the very beginning that a letter was the last thing I expected. Letters are things I receive three times a year: one from my landlord, to ask for the rent; one from my banker, to inform me that I am in a position to pay it; one, on New Year's Day, . . . I prefer not to tell you from whom. The address was written in an unknown hand. The absolute lack of character which was afterwards revealed to me by this handwriting, through the assistance of graphologists whom I consulted, was such that I could learn nothing further. They found in it no characteristics whatsoever, except an extreme kind-heartedness; though some of them preferred to diagnose this as weakness. They could say nothing definite. Please remember that I speak only of the writing on the envelope, for there was none inside; no, none at all—not a line, not a word. Inside the envelope there was nothing but a five hundred franc note.

I was about to drink my morning cup of chocolate; but my astonishment was so great that I let it get cold. I racked my brains . . . no one owed me anything. I have a fixed income, gentlemen, and I contrive to put by enough each year to compensate, more or less, for the regular fall in the value of my shares. As I've already said, I wasn't expecting anything. I have never asked for anything. Habituation to my very regular mode of existence prevented me from even wishing for anything. I pondered a great deal, in accordance with the best methods of enquiry: *Cur, unde, quo, qua?*—Whence, wherefore, how, why? And this five hundred franc note was no answer to my questions, since until I received it I hadn't even begun to ask them.

I thought: no doubt it's a mistake; well, now I shall be able to rectify it. This money was intended for some-one else with the same name. So I looked in the Directory for some namesake, who perhaps was already expecting it to arrive. But my name isn't a very usual one nowa-days; I saw, as I turned over that enormous volume's leaves, that I was the only one it mentioned. I thought the writing on the envelope might lead me to a better result, and help me to find, if not the addressee, the sender. It was then that I had recourse to the graphologists. But no—they could tell me nothing; I only succeeded in aggravating my troubles. Those five hundred francs weigh heavier upon me every day: I would like to get rid of them, and I don't know how. Because after all . . . And besides, if anyone gave them me intentionally, at least he deserves my gratitude. Grateful—I am only too anxious to be grateful—but I don't know to whom.

In the hope of some new accident to relieve me of my trouble, I carry the five hundred francs note on my per-son. I never leave it, day or night. I am its property.— Before, I was commonplace but free. Now I belong to the banknote. This adventure has determined my iden-tity: I used to be a nobody, now I am somebody.

Ever since then, I have changed my way of life; I

keep looking for someone to talk to, and the reason why I very frequently sit down to eat in this restaurant is that, thanks to these tables for three, I hope some day to find, in one of the two companions offered me, a person who will recognize the handwriting on the envelope—and here it is. . . ."

As he uttered these words, Damocles drew a sigh from his bosom and a dirty yellow envelope from his coat-pocket. On it sprawled the letters of his name, written in an undistinguished hand. Then the following strange event occurred: Cocles, who till then had remained silent, continued to be so—but raised against Damocles a fist which the waiter had just time to halt in mid-air. Cocles was thus enabled to recover his self-possession, and to say in a mournful voice these words, which his companions only understood some time later:

"After all, it's better as it is, for if I'd returned the slap in the face, you would have thought yourself obliged to return the banknote, and . . . it doesn't belong to me."— Then, as Damocles seemed to await some explanation of his gesture: "It was I," he added, pointing to the envelope, "who wrote your address on this."

"But how did you know my name?" said Damocles, who was disposed to take the incident in bad part.

"By the merest chance—" said Cocles quietly: "—however, that is of little importance in this affair. My story is still more curious than yours; allow me to tell it you, in as few words as possible:"

THE STORY OF COCLES

My acquaintances on this earth are few; in fact, before the event I am about to relate to you, I was unaware that

I had any. I do not know who brought me into the world, and I have long been seeking some reason for continuing to live. I went out into the street in quest of some external event that might help me to a decision. I thought my destiny would depend on the first thing that happened to me; for I am not responsible for my own making, being too naturally kindhearted for that. I felt convinced that my very first action would motivate my existence. Since I am naturally kindhearted, as I have already said, this action consisted in picking up a hand-kerchief from the pavement. The person who let it drop had only had time to walk two or three steps away; I ran after him and handed it back. He took it without showing any surprise; no—the surprise was mine, when I saw him hold out an envelope, the very one that you see here. "Be so kind," said he with a smile, "as to write an address on this envelope." "Whose?" I asked. "Anybody's," he replied.—Saying this, he offered me all the necessary materials for writing.—Having no desire to withdraw myself from exterior motivation, I obeyed. But, as I have already assured you, my acquaintances on this earth are few. The name I wrote, which came into my head I don't know how, was that of a perfect stranger. This done, I bowed to him, thinking my part was finished, and I was about to continue my way, when I received an appalling blow in the face.

The amazement this caused me did not allow me to notice what became of my assailant. When I came to myself again, I was surrounded by a crowd of people. Everybody was speaking at once. Some had taken hold of me and were trying to carry me to the nearby chemist's. I could only tear myself away from their attentions by assuring them that I was quite unhurt, although in reality my nose was bleeding and I had a violent pain in my jaw.

The inflammation of my cheek kept me a whole week in my room.

I spent this time in pondering:

Why did he give me that slap in the face?

No doubt it was by mistake. What grudge could he possibly have against me? I have never done evil to a living soul; and no one could wish me any; evil is a thing one does in return.

And supposing it wasn't a mistake, I thought (for up to then I hadn't been able to think); supposing this slap in the face really was meant for me! But then I added: Ah well, what does it matter! whether by mistake or not, I had it, and . . . and shall I give it back?—As I have said already, I am by nature kindhearted; and besides, there was one thing that embarrassed me: the person who hit me was stronger than I am.

When the pain in my cheek had subsided and I was able to go out at last, I tried to find my assailant again, I confess; yes, but it was in order to avoid him. In any case, I never met him, and if I succeeded in avoiding him, it was without knowing it.

But"—and as he said this he leaned towards Prometheus—"see how to-day everything somehow links up, yet instead of explaining itself becomes still more complicated:—I learn now that thanks to my blow in the face, this gentleman has received five hundred francs. . . ."

"Oh! but excuse me!" said Damocles.

"My name is Cocles, sir," said he, bowing to Damocles; "Cocles! and I tell you my name, Damocles, in the certainty that you will be glad to know to whom you owe your windfall. . . ."

"But . . ."

"Yes.—I know what you are about to remark. Let's not say 'to whom,' but 'to whose suffering.' . . . For you must realize, and never forget, that your gain was at the expense of my misfortune. . . ."

"But . . ."

"Do not argue the point, if you please. Between your gain and my misfortune there is a relationship; I don't know what, but the relationship exists. . . ."

"But, sir . . ."

"Don't call me sir."

"But, my dear Cocles."

"Call me just Cocles."

"But once again, my good Cocles . . ."

"No, sir—no, Damocles—and whatever you may say, it will be no use, for I bear the mark of the blow on my cheek to this day . . . there's a scar, which I will now proceed to show you."

The conversation was becoming disagreeably personal. It was here that the waiter's sense of tact came to light.

IV

By a skilful manœuvre—merely by upsetting a plate of food on Prometheus—he turned upon the latter the sudden attention of the two others. Prometheus, was unable to keep back an exclamation, and his voice, after that of his companions, at once seemed so deep that they became aware that until then he had kept silent.

The irritation of Damocles and Cocles joined forces.

"But you aren't saying anything——" they exclaimed.

PROMETHEUS SPEAKS

"Gentlemen, anything I could say would have so little relevance. . . . I don't even see how . . . in fact, the more I think of it . . . No, really, I can't possibly say anything. Each of you has his own story; I have none. You must excuse me. Please believe it was with unmixed interest that I heard each of you telling an adventure which I would like only too well . . . to be able . . . But I can't even express myself with ease. No, really, you will have to be so kind as to excuse me, my dear sirs: it is hardly two hours since I came to Paris. There hasn't been time yet for anything to happen to me—except your invaluable acquaintance, which makes me feel most keenly what

a Parisian conversation can be, when clever people begin
to . . ."

"But before you came here," said Cocles.

"You must have been somewhere else," said Damocles.

"Yes, I admit it," said Prometheus, "but, I repeat, all
that is quite irrelevant to . . ."

"It doesn't matter," said Cocles, "we've come here to
talk. Both of us, Damocles and I, have already brought
out our story; you alone make no contribution; you
only listen; it isn't right. It is time for you to speak,
Mr. . . ."

The waiter felt with all his tact that it was time for an
introduction, and, slipping the name in as if to complete
the previous phrase:

"Prometheus——" he said simply.

"Prometheus," resumed Damocles.—"Excuse me,
sir, but it seems to me that this name has already . . ."

"Oh!" interrupted Prometheus immediately, "that is
of no importance whatsoever."

"But, if nothing is important," cried the other two
impatiently, "why have you come here, my dear Mr. . . .
Mr. . . .?"

"Prometheus," repeated Prometheus simply.

"My dear Mr. Prometheus—for after all, as I had
occasion to remark just now," continued Cocles, "this
restaurant invites conversation, and in any case, nothing
will persuade me to believe that the peculiar name
you bear is the only thing that marks you out from
others; if you haven't done anything yet, you must
mean to do something soon; what are you capable of
doing? Show us your distinguishing characteristics: what
have you that no one else has? Why do they call you
Prometheus?"

Under this deluge of questions Prometheus bowed his

head, and was obliged to reply, submissively and in a tone graver than before, though still confusedly:

"You ask what I have, gentlemen?—What I have, I personally, is—ahem! an eagle."

"A what?"

"An eagle—or a vulture, perhaps—people aren't quite sure."

"An eagle! That's a good one!—an eagle . . . where is it, then?"

"You really insist on seeing it?" said Prometheus.

"Yes," they said, "if it isn't being indiscreet."

Then, all too completely forgetting where he was, Prometheus abruptly rose to his feet and uttered a great cry of summons to his mighty eagle. And there occurred the stupefying event that follows:

THE STORY OF THE EAGLE

A bird, which seemed enormous from a distance, but at close quarters was seen to be not so large after all, darkened for a moment the sky above the boulevard, fell like a tornado in the direction of the café, smashed the plate-glass window, and alighted—dashing Cocles' eye out with a blow of its wing, and uttering a shower of affectionate but none the less imperious chirrups— alighted, I say, on the right hip of Prometheus.

The latter immediately unbuttoned his waistcoat and offered a morsel of his liver to the bird.

V

There was a tremendous uproar in the café.

The voices lost all community of opinion and began to diverge—for by this time other people had come upon the scene.

"Well, I say, look out, you know," said Cocles.

His objection was drowned by the most insistent element of the tumult, which said:

"That, an eagle! Come, come now! !—Just take a look at the poor moth-eaten creature! That . . . an eagle! Come, come now! ! It's nothing but a conscience, at the the very most."

The fact is, the great eagle was a pitiable object; thin, flapping its wings, with half its feathers missing, ravening greedily on its tortured pittance, you could see the poor bird hadn't eaten for the last three days.

Others however showed more assiduity, and said to Prometheus in a lower voice, insinuatingly: "But, my good sir, you mustn't think this eagle distinguishes you in any way. An eagle, when all's said and done, if you don't mind my saying so, is what we all of us have."

"But . . ." said he.

"But we don't wear it in Paris," they continued . . . "In Paris it is extremely out of place. An eagle is a nuisance. Just take a look at what it has done! If it amuses

121

you to give it your liver to eat, you can please yourself; but allow me to point out that it is a painful sight for others to watch. If you must do it, do it in private."

And Prometheus murmured, covered in confusion: "Please excuse me, gentlemen—oh! really, I'm most awfully sorry. What shall I do?"

"But one gets rid of it before coming in, sir."

And some said: "One wrings its neck."

While the rest said: "One advertises it for sale.— That is what newspaper offices are for, sir."

And in the growing uproar no one noticed Damocles, who suddenly asked the waiter for the bill.

The waiter handed him the following:

Three lunches inclusive (with conversation) . .	30 francs	
One plate-glass window .	450 „	
One glass eye for Cocles .	3.50	

". . . and keep the change for yourself," said Damocles, slipping the banknote into the waiter's hand. Then he fled, blissfully.

The end of this chapter can present only a much inferior interest to the reader. All that happened was, that the restaurant gradually emptied. Prometheus and Cocles demanded their share of the bill in vain: Damocles had paid for everything.

Prometheus took leave of the waiter and of Cocles, and as he slowly wended his way back to the Caucasus, he pondered: "Shall I sell it?—shall I wring its neck? . . . or should I tame it, perhaps? . . ."

PROMETHEUS IN PRISON

A FEW DAYS LATER Prometheus, denounced by the friendly care of the waiter, found himself put in prison for manufacturing matches without a licence.

The prison was isolated from the rest of the world, and nothing could be seen from it but the sky; from outside it had the appearance of a tower; inside, Prometheus was plunged in boredom.

The waiter came to call on him.

"Oh!" Prometheus said to him, with a smile, "how delighted I am to see you! I was pining away. Speak to me, you who come from the outside world; the wall of this cell cuts me off from it, and I no longer know anything of other men. What are they doing? And, first of all, what are *you* doing?"

"Since your scandal broke out," replied the waiter, "hardly anything; we've had scarcely any customers. We've had to waste a great deal of time repairing the plate-glass window."

"I am terribly sorry to hear it," said Prometheus; "—but Damocles, now? Have you seen Damocles again? He left the restaurant in such a hurry the other day; I hadn't time to say goodbye to him. I regret it. He seemed a very nice person, full of decency and scruples; he told us his troubles so artlessly, and it touched me. I hope, at least, he had recovered his composure when he left the table?"

"It didn't last long," said the waiter. "I saw him again the next day, and his anxiety was worse than ever. While he was talking to me he burst into tears. What troubles him most of all, is Cocles' state of health."

"Is he very ill, then?" asked Prometheus.

"Cocles? Why, no," replied the waiter. "I'd go so far as to say that he sees all the better, now he has only one eye to see with. He shows his glass eye to everybody, and he's as happy as can be when they commiserate with him. When you see him again, tell him that his new eye suits him perfectly, and that he wears it with a certain grace; but then add that he must have suffered terribly. . . ."

"Does he suffer, then?"

"Yes, perhaps—when people don't tell him that he does."

"But then, if Cocles is in the best of health, and doesn't suffer at all, what has Damocles to worry about?"

"About the terrible way Cocles ought to have suffered."

"But that's exactly what you recommend me to tell him. . . ."

"To tell him, yes, but Damocles really believes it, and it's killing him."

"What else does he do?"

"Nothing. This one preoccupation monopolizes him. Between ourselves, he's a man with an obsession.—He says that if it hadn't been for those five hundred francs, Cocles wouldn't be so unhappy."

"And Cocles?"

"He says the same. . . . But he has become very rich."

126

"How so?"

"Oh! I don't quite know;—but they've shown him a good deal of sympathy in the newspapers; they've opened a subscription in his favour."

"And what's he doing with it?"

"He's a crafty one. With the money that the collection has brought in, he's thinking of founding a hospital."

"A hospital?"

"Yes, a small one; just for people who've lost an eye. He's had himself made governor."

"Aha!" cried Prometheus; "you interest me enormously."

"I hoped I would," said the waiter.

"And now, tell me . . . the Miglionaire?"

"Oh! he's a cool one!—If you think he's losing any sleep over all this! ! He's like me: he just observes . . . If it would amuse you, I'll introduce you to him—when you're out."

"Yes, that reminds me, why am I in?" Prometheus at last began. "Of what do they accuse me? Do you know that, waiter, you who know so many things?"

"No, upon my honour," said the waiter mendaciously. "At least, what I do know is, that so far you've only been remanded in custody. After they've sentenced you, then you'll know."

"Well, so much the better!" said Prometheus; "I always prefer to know."

"Goodbye," the waiter said next; "it's getting late. It's amazing how quickly time passes when I'm with you. . . . But tell me: your eagle? what's become of it?"

"I say! I haven't given it a thought," said Prometheus. And, when the waiter had left, Prometheus began to think about his eagle.

IT MUST INCREASE BUT I MUST DECREASE

And, as Prometheus was feeling bored to tears, when evening fell he called his eagle.—And the eagle came.

"I've been waiting for you for ages," said Prometheus.

"Then why didn't you call me sooner?" replied the eagle.

For the first time Prometheus looked at his eagle, as it perched unceremoniously on the twisted bars of his cell. In the golden light of the setting sun it looked dingier than ever. It was grey, ugly, haggard, sulky, resigned and woebegone. It seemed too weak to fly; seeing which, Prometheus wept from pity for his eagle.

"Faithful bird," said he, "you seem in pain—tell me: what is the matter?"

"I'm hungry," said the eagle.

"Eat," said Prometheus, uncovering his liver.

The bird ate.

"You're hurting me," said Prometheus.

But the eagle said nothing more that day.

II

Next day, as soon as dawn broke, Prometheus began
to miss his eagle; he summoned it from the red glow of
the morning sky, and, as the sun appeared, the eagle
came. It had three feathers more than on the previous
day. Prometheus sobbed with affection.

"How long it took you to come," said he, caressing its
plumage.

"That's because I can't fly very fast yet," said the bird.
"I can only just clear the ground."

"Why?"

"I'm so weak."

"What do you need, to fly fast?"

"Your liver."

"Here you are then; eat."

Next day the eagle had eight more feathers; and a few
days later it outstripped the dawn. But Prometheus, on
the other hand, was growing thin.

"Talk to me about the outside world," Prometheus
said to it, "what's become of the others?"

"Oh! I soar high in the air now," replied the eagle;
"I know nothing, except the sky and you."

Its wings had grown gradually broader and longer.

"Beautiful bird, what have you to tell me this morning?"

"I have flown with my hunger to the ends of space."

"Eagle! will you never be less cruel?"

"No! But I may become very beautiful."

Prometheus, falling in love with the future beauty of his eagle, gave it more and more to eat every day.

One evening, the eagle did not go.

Next day it was still there.

Neither left the other idle for a moment; the bird bit the prisoner, while the prisoner fondled the bird, growing lean and spent with love, caressing its plumage all day and sleeping all night beneath its wing, feeding it to its heart's content.—The eagle never left him, either by night or by day.

"Sweet eagle! Who would have believed it?"

"Believed what?"

"That our love-affair would be so delightful."

"Ah! Prometheus . . ."

"Tell me, for you know it, my sweetest eagle, why am I in prison?"

"What does it matter? Am I not with you?"

"Yes; it matters little, indeed! Still, are you satisfied with me, beautiful eagle?"

"Yes, if you think me very beautiful."

III

Spring came; round the bars of the prison twined sweet-scented honeysuckle in flower.

"One day we'll go away," said the eagle.

"Do you mean it?" cried Prometheus.

"Because I've become very strong, and you, very thin; and I can carry you away."

"Eagle, my eagle . . . carry me away."

And the eagle flew away with Prometheus.

A CHAPTER TO KEEP THE READER WAITING FOR THE NEXT

That evening Cocles and Damocles met. They entered into conversation, but there was certainly some embarrassment between them.

"It can't be helped," said Cocles, "our points of view are diametrically opposite."

"Do you think so?" replied Damocles. "I ask nothing better than for us to speak with one voice."

"That's what you say, but you don't hear any voice but your own."

"And as for you, you don't even listen to mine. Tell me, then, what I ought to do, if you know it."

"You claim to know it better than I do."

"Alas! Cocles, you're losing your temper; but, for the love of heaven, tell me: what must I do?"

"Well, don't do anything more for me, if you please; you've already given me a glass eye . . ."

"Only because I couldn't give you a better one, my good Cocles."

"No—not after you'd blinded me."

"But that wasn't me, my dear Cocles."

"It was the very least you could do for me; and besides you had the money to pay for it—thanks to my slap in the face."

"Cocles! let's forget the past."

"Oh yes! it suits you to forget it."

"That isn't at all what I meant to say."

"But what do you mean to say, then? Come now, speak up!"

"You won't listen to me."

"That's because I know just what you're going to say!"

For want of any fresh subject to change its course, their discussion was about to take an unpleasant turn, when they both suddenly collided with a man carrying a sandwich-board. On it they could read:

THIS EVENING AT 8 O'CLOCK

IN THE
HALL OF BLUE MOONS
PROMETHEUS UNBOUND
WILL LECTURE ON
HIS EAGLE

At half-past eight
**The Eagle will come on and do
some tricks**

At nine o'clock
**The waiter will take a collection in aid of
the Cocles Hospital**

"That will be worth seeing," said Cocles.
"I'll go with you," said Damocles.

IV

At eight o'clock sharp the crowd entered the Hall of Blue Moons.

Cocles sat in the centre on the left, Damocles in the centre on the right; the rest of the public between them.

A thunder of applause greeted the entry of Prometheus; he ascended the steps of the platform, put down his eagle at his side, and gathered himself together. In the hall there was a thrilling silence. . . .

BEGGING THE QUESTION

"Gentlemen," began Prometheus, "having, alas, no expectation of interesting you in what I am about to say, I have taken the precaution of bringing this eagle with me. After every tedious portion of my discourse, it will be so kind as to perform a few tricks for us. Moreover, I have with me some obscene photographs and some sky-rockets; at the most serious parts of my lecture I shall take care to amuse the public with them. I venture, therefore, gentlemen, to hope for some attention on your part.

At each new point in my speech, I shall have the honour, gentlemen, of inviting you to witness my eagle taking a meal; for my lecture, gentlemen, has three points; (I felt there was no need to reject this style of construction, which suits my classical turn of mind.)— And with this as an exordium, I will now announce, in advance and without meretricious disguise, the first two points of my discourse:

First point: Everyone should have an eagle.

Second point: We all have one anyway.

Fearing lest you should accuse me of making up my mind in advance, gentlemen, fearing also lest I should impair the liberty of my thought, I have not prepared my discourse beyond this stage; my third point will devolve naturally from the two others; in arriving at it I mean to let the passion of the moment have full play.—And by way of conclusion, the eagle, gentlemen, will take the collection."

"Bravo! Bravo!" cried Cocles.

Prometheus drank a mouthful of water. The eagle pirouetted three times round Prometheus, and then bowed. Prometheus looked at the audience, smiled at Damocles and Cocles, and then, as no sign of boredom was visible as yet, postponed his rockets till later, and continued:

V

"Whatever rhetorical skill I brought to bear, gentlemen, I should never succeed in concealing from your
perspicacious intelligence the fatal begging of the
question, which lies in wait for me at the very beginning
of my discourse.

Gentlemen, whatever our efforts, we shall never escape
from begging the question. What does it mean, to beg the
question? Gentlemen, if I may venture to say so, begging
the question is always an assertion of temperament; for
it is unprincipled to beg, and where principles are lacking,
assertion of temperament steps in.

When I declare: everyone should have an eagle, all of
you might well exclaim: Why?—Now, is there any
answer I could give you, which might not be reduced to
this formula, in which my temperament asserts itself: I
do not love men: I love what devours them.

Temperament, gentlemen, may be defined as 'that
which must be asserted.' He's begging the question again,
you will say. But I have just declared that begging the
question is always an assertion of temperament; and as I
say that temperament must be asserted, I repeat: I do not
love Man; I love what devours him.—Now, what
devours Man?—His eagle. Therefore, gentlemen, everyone should have an eagle. This point, I think, needs no
further demonstration.

. . . Alas! I see, gentlemen, that I am boring you; certain persons are beginning to yawn. I could, it is true, make a few jokes at this point; but you would feel they were being dragged in; I have an incurably serious turn of mind. I prefer to distribute some indecent photographs; they will cause those of you who are being bored by my words to hold their peace: and that will permit me to continue."

Prometheus drank a mouthful of water. The eagle pirouetted three times round Prometheus, and then bowed. Prometheus went on:

PROMETHEUS' LECTURE CONTINUED

"Gentlemen, I have not always known my eagle. That is what makes me infer, by a form of reasoning which has a special name that I can't recall for the moment, as I have only been studying logic during the past week— that, I was saying, is what makes me infer, although the only eagle to be seen here is my own, that an eagle, gentlemen, is something all of you have.

Up till now I have kept silence concerning my story— besides, until now I did not quite understand it myself. And if I now decide to speak of it to you, it is because, thanks to my eagle, it now seems to me miraculously wonderful.

VI

"Gentlemen, as I have told you, I have not always seen my eagle. Before I saw it, I was careless and handsome, happy and naked without knowing it. Delightful days! On the gushing flanks of Caucasus, happy and naked as myself, the voluptuous Asia embraced me. Together we tumbled in the valleys; our senses were filled with the singing of the air, the laughter of the water, the fragrance of the meanest flowers that blow. Often we lay together under the spreading branches, among flowers where murmuring swarms brushed wing with wing. Asia, full of laughter, became my bride; and then the sounds of humming swarms and rustling leaves, mingling with the ripple of innumerable streams, invited us softly to the softest of slumbers. Everything around us gave permission and protection to our inhuman solitude.— Suddenly, one day, Asia said to me: "You ought to pay some attention to human beings."

First of all I had to go and find them.

I was only too willing to pay attention to them; but all I could do was pity them.

They were extremely unenlightened; I invented various forms of fire for them; and from that day forth my eagle began. Ever since then I have been aware of my nakedness."

At these words applause broke out in different parts of the hall. Prometheus abruptly burst into tears. The eagle clapped its wings and cooed. With a terrible gesture Prometheus unbuttoned his waistcoat and offered his wincing liver to the bird. The applause was redoubled. Then the eagle pirouetted three times round Prometheus; the latter drank a mouthful of water, gathered himself together, and continued his discourse in the following terms:

VII

"Gentlemen, my modesty carried me away; forgive me: this is the first time I have spoken in public. But now it is my candour that carries me away: gentlemen, I have paid far more attention to men than I told you just now. Gentlemen, I have done a very great deal for men. Gentlemen, I have loved men passionately, desperately and deplorably.—And I have given them so much, that I might just as well say that I have given them their being; for what were they previously?—They existed, but they weren't conscious of existing. Like a fire for their enlightenment, gentlemen, out of all my love for them I made them this consciousness.—The first conscience they ever had, was that of their beauty. That is what made possible the propagation of the species. Man prolonged himself in his posterity. The beauty of the forerunners repeated itself, equal, indifferent, and without history. That might have gone on indefinitely. Then I became anxious; already bearing within me, without knowing it, the egg of my eagle, I wanted something more, or something better. This propagation, this piece-meal prolongation seemed to me to indicate in them a state of waiting—whereas in reality it was only my eagle that was waiting. I knew nothing of this; I believed this state of waiting was inside man; in fact, it was I that put it inside them. Now, of course, because I had made man in my own image, I understand that in each man something that hadn't yet opened out was lying in wait; in each one of them there was the eagle's egg. . . . And yet, I don't know; I can't quite explain all that.—What I do know is that, not satisfied with giving them consciousness of their existence, I wanted to give them also a reason for existing. I gave them fire, flame, and all the arts whose nutriment is a flame. Warming their spirits within them, gentlemen, I brought into existence the devouring belief in progress. And I rejoiced strangely, that man's health should be spent in producing it.— No more belief in good, but a sick hope for better. Belief in progress, gentlemen, was their eagle. Our eagle is our reason for existing, gentlemen.

Man's happiness grew less and less, and it was all one to me: the eagle was born. Gentlemen, I loved men no more, it was what lived through and on them that I loved. I had finished with a humanity without a history. . . . The history of mankind is the history of eagles, gentlemen. . . ."

VIII

Here there were some bursts of applause. Prometheus rather bashfully continued:

"Gentlemen, I was not speaking the truth: forgive me: it didn't happen as quickly as that: no, I have not always loved eagles: for a long time I preferred mankind; its injured happiness was dear to me, for, having tampered with it, I believed I had become responsible for it, and every time I thought of this, in the evening, my eagle came, gloomy as a remorse, to take his food.

At this time he was lean and grey of hue, anxious, morose; he was as ugly as a vulture.—Gentlemen, look at him now, and you will understand why I am talking; why I have assembled you here, and why I entreat you to listen to me: it is because I have made this discovery: it is possible for the eagle to become very beautiful. Now each of you has an eagle: I have just assured you of the fact. An eagle? Alas, perhaps a vulture! No, no! Not a vulture, gentlemen!—Gentlemen, everyone must have an eagle. . . .

And now I touch upon the most serious question:— why the eagle! Ah! why?—it must give the answer itself. Here is mine, gentlemen, I bring it to you. . . . Eagle! will you answer me, now? . . ."

Anxiously, Prometheus turned to his eagle. The eagle was motionless and remained silent . . . Prometheus continued in a voice full of grief:

"Gentlemen, I have questioned my eagle in vain . . .
Eagle! do speak now: everyone is listening . . . Who
sent you?—Why did you choose me? Where do you
come from? Where are you going? Tell me: what is your
nature? . . . (The eagle remained silent)—No, nothing!
not a word! not a cry! I thought it would speak, if not
to me, at least, to you; that's why I brought it . . .
Shall I have to do all the talking here? All is silence!
All is silence!—What's to be said! . . . I have asked in
vain."

Then, turning towards the assembly, he said: "Oh!
I hoped, gentlemen, that you would love my eagle, that
your love would give its beauty a reason for existing.—
That's why I abandoned myself to it, gorged it with the
blood of my soul . . . but I see I am alone in admiring
it . . . Oh! isn't it enough for you that it is beautiful?—
or do you dispute the fact of its beauty? Do look at it,
at least. . . . I have lived for nothing else—and now I
bring it to you: behold it!—I lived for it—but for what
does it live?—Eagle! Eagle that I fed with my blood,
with my soul, that I caressed with all my love . . . (here
Prometheus was interrupted by his own sobbing)—
must I then leave this earth without knowing why I
loved you? or what you will do, or what you will be,
when I am gone, on this earth . . . this earth . . . I have
asked in vain . . . asked in vain."

The phrase was strangled in his throat; tears prevented
his voice from carrying.

"Forgive me, gentlemen," he went on, a little more
calmly; "—forgive me for speaking of such serious matters; but if I knew any more serious still, it would be of
those that I would speak."

Bathed in sweat, Prometheus wiped his face, drank a
mouthful of water, and added:

PROMETHEUS' LECTURE CONCLUDED

"That is as far as I have prepared . . ."

At these words there was a violent eddy of protest in the hall; several persons who were bored beyond endurance tried to leave.

"Gentlemen," cried Prometheus, "—I entreat you to remain here; it won't be very long now; but the most important part is still to come, if I haven't persuaded you already . . . Gentlemen!—for heaven's sake . . . See here! quickly—here are some fireworks; and I'm keeping the very best ones for the end . . .

Gentlemen! Sit down again, for pity's sake; just look: do you think I'm trying to economize? I'm lighting six at a time!—And while we're about it, waiter, have the doors closed."

The fireworks had quite a good effect. Almost everyone who had got up sat down again.

"But now, where was I?" resumed Prometheus. "I was counting on gathering enough impetus to carry me through, and your movement has stopped it. . . ."

"Well, so much the better," someone shouted.

"Ah! I know . . ." continued Prometheus, "—I wanted to tell you yet again . . ."

("—Enough! Enough!!" came shouts from every direction.)

". . . That you must all love your eagle."

Several ironical cries of "Why" were uttered.

"I can hear, gentlemen, that I am being asked 'why?': I answer: because then it will become beautiful."

"But if it makes us ugly!"

"Gentlemen, what I offer you here is not a message of interest . . ."

"We can tell that for ourselves!"

"It's a message of devotion. Gentlemen, we must devote ourselves to our eagle. . . . (Agitation; many people rose to their feet.) Gentlemen! Don't get up, now: I'm going to bring personalities in . . . There's no need to remind you who are here about the story of Cocles and Damocles. You all know it already; well then! I say this to their faces: the secret of their life is in their devotion to their debt; yours, Cocles, to your slap in the face; yours, Damocles, to your banknote. Cocles, you had to gash your scar and empty your eyesocket, O Cocles; you, Damocles, had to keep your five hundred francs, and continue to owe them without shame, and owe still more, and take joy in owing. That was your eagle; there are others; there are some that are more glorious. But I tell you this: the eagle, whatever it be, devours us, vice or virtue, duty or passion; once you cease to be a mere nobody, you will never escape it. But . . ."

(Here the voice of Prometheus almost vanished in the uproar) "—but if you do not feed your eagle with love, it will remain grey of hue, pitiable, invisible to everyone and deceitful; then people will call it a mere conscience, unworthy of the torments it causes; they will say it has no beauty.—Gentlemen, we must love our eagle, love it in order that it may grow beautiful; for it's because it will become beautiful, that you must love your eagle. I have finished now, gentlemen, my eagle will proceed to take the collection; gentlemen, you must love my eagle.— All the same, I will let off a few squibs."

.   .   .   .

.   .   .   .

Thanks to this pyrotechnic diversion, the meeting ended without undue disturbance; but Damocles caught cold leaving the hall.

DAMOCLES IS ILL

I

"YOU KNOW, HE's in a bad way," said the waiter, when he saw Prometheus again several days later. "Who?"

"Damocles—oh! in a very bad way:—he caught it on his way out after your lecture . . ."

"It? What?"

"The doctors can't make out;—it's such a rare disease . . . they say it's a stricture of the column. . . ."

"The column?"

"The column. If he isn't saved by a sudden miracle, the trouble's bound to get worse. He's sinking, I assure you, and you ought to go and see him."

"Do you visit him often?"

"Oh yes, every day. He's worried about Cocles; so I bring all the news about him."

"Why doesn't he go there himself?"

"Cocles?—He's too busy. Your speech, didn't you know? had an extraordinary effect on him. He talks about nothing but devoting himself, and spends all his time looking round the streets for a new slap in the face to bring in money to some new Damocles. He keeps holding out the other cheek in vain."

"You must warn the Miglionaire."

"I keep him informed daily. In fact that is why I go to see Damocles every day."

"Why doesn't he go himself?"

"That's what I tell him, but he refuses. He doesn't want to be known. And yet, Damocles would recover if he knew his benefactor: I tell him so, but he persists; he wants to keep his incognito—and I realize now that it isn't Damocles, but his illness, that interests him."

"You spoke of introducing me . . .?"

"This very moment, if you like."

So they went there without more ado.

II

Not having known him personally, we have promised ourselves to speak only briefly of Zeus, the waiter's friend.

Let us report simply these few phrases.

INTERVIEW WITH THE MIGLIONAIRE

The Waiter: Isn't it true that you are very wealthy?

The Miglionaire, half turning to Prometheus: I am a great deal wealthier than anyone can imagine. You belong to me; he belongs to me; everything belongs to me.— You think I am a banker; I am something quite different. My influence cn Paris is hidden, but it isn't any the less important. It is hidden because I don't go through with it. Yes, mine is, above all, the spirit of initiative. I simply launch. Then, when a business is launched, I leave it; I don't touch it again.

The Waiter: Isn't it true that your actions are gratuitous?

The Miglionaire: I alone, he alone whose fortune is infinite, can act with absolute disinterestedness; man cannot. Hence my love of gambling; not of gain, you understand me, but of gambling; what could I gain that

I don't possess already? Not even time . . . Do you know how old I am?

Prometheus and the Waiter: You seem young still, sir.

The Miglionaire: Then please refrain from interrupting me, Prometheus. Yes, gambling is my passion. I gamble by lending to men.—I lend, but only by way of a game. I lend, but only to insolvents who can never pay me back; I lend, but in such a way that I seem to give outright.— I like people not to know that I lend. I play, but no one ever sees my hand. I experiment; I lay my stakes like a Dutchman planting his secret bulb. What I lend to Man, what I plant in him, grows—and how that amuses me! It amuses me to watch it growing. Without that, Man would be so empty!—Let me tell you about my most recent experiment. You shall help me to observe it. First of all, listen to me, and you will understand afterwards. Oh yes, you will understand.

I went down to the street, looking for a way to make someone suffer for the gift I was going to make to someone else; to make this other profit from the harm I would do to that one. All I needed was a slap and a five hundred franc note. The one got the slap, the other got the banknote. Is that quite clear? But what is less clear is the method of distribution.

"I know how it was done," interrupted Prometheus.

"Eh? What? You know?" said Zeus.

"I met Damocles and Cocles; it is precisely about them that I have come to speak to you: Damocles is looking for you and calling for you; he is anxious; he is ill; for pity's sake, show yourself to him."

"Sir, let us say no more on this subject," said Zeus— "I am not in the habit of taking advice from anyone."

"Told you so!" said the waiter.

Prometheus was about to go, but suddenly changing

his mind again, he said: "Sir, I beg your pardon. Excuse the indiscretion of this request. Oh! Show it me, I entreat you! I should so like to see it. . . ."

"What?"

"Your eagle."

"But I have no eagle, sir."

"No eagle? He hasn't an eagle! ! But . . ."

"No more than in the flat of my hand! Eagles! (and Zeus laughed) why, it's I who give them to others."

Prometheus was overcome with amazement.

"Do you know what they say?" the waiter asked the banker.

"What do they say?"

"That you are God Almighty."

"I have no objection to their saying so," he said.

III

Prometheus went to see Damocles; and then, after the first time, went often. He did not speak to him every time; but at least the waiter gave him news of the patient. One day he took Cocles with him.

The waiter let them in.

"Well! How is he to-day?" asked Prometheus.

"Bad. Very bad," replied the waiter. "For the last three days the poor soul hasn't been able to keep anything down. He's tormented with wondering what has happened to his banknote; he looks everywhere for it, and can't find it anywhere; he believes he has eaten it and takes purges because he thinks he might find it in his stools. When he recovers his reason and remembers his adventure, he only mopes worse than ever. He bears a grudge against you, Cocles, because he says you complicate his debt, so that now he can't make head or tail of it. Most of the time he's raving. At night there are three of us to watch him, but he leaps up and down on his bed, and that prevents us from sleeping."

"Do you think we could see him?" said Cocles.

"Yes, but you'll find him changed. He's eaten up with anxiety. He is thin as thin can be. I doubt whether you'll recognize him even.—Besides, will he recognize you?"

They went in on tip-toe.

THE LAST DAYS OF DAMOCLES

Damocles' bedroom smelled disgustingly of medicine. It had a low ceiling and was very narrow. It was lit funereally by two night-lights. In the alcove, under a hideous pile of bedclothes, Damocles could be dimly seen tossing and turning. He was speaking to someone at random, although there was no one to listen to him; his voice was hoarse and muffled. Prometheus and Cocles looked at one another, full of horror; Damocles, without hearing them approach, continued, as if he was alone: "And from that day forward," he was saying, "I felt, at one and the same time, that my life had acquired a meaning, and that I could no longer bear to live. Those hateful, accursed five hundred francs!—I felt I owed them to everyone, and dared not give them to anyone—because then I would have deprived all the others of them. My only thought was to get rid of them—but how?—the savings-bank!—but that meant increasing my trouble; the burden of my debt was made heavier by all the interest on it; and besides, the idea of letting the money stagnate was unbearable; so I carried it always on my person; regularly, once a week, I changed the banknote for coins, then the coins for another banknote. But one neither gains nor loses by exchanging; it's simply a form of circular madness. And added to all that was this tormenting thought: it's thanks to another's slap in the face that I possess these five hundred francs!—One day, as you know, I met you in the restaurant . . ."

"He's talking about you now," said the waiter.

"Prometheus' eagle smashed a plate-glass window, knocked Cocles' eye out. . . . Hurrah! I'm saved! ! Gratuitously, fortuitously, providentially, I'll slip my money into the gap between these events. No more debt!

I'm saved! Ah! Gentlemen! what a mistake . . . It was
from that day that my agony began. How can I explain
this to you? Will you ever understand my anguish?
These five hundred francs, I owe them still, and I no
longer even possess them! I have tried, like a coward, to
get rid of my debt, but I have not discharged it. In the
nightmares that come to me every night, I wake bathed
in sweat, I kneel, I cry aloud: "Lord! Lord! to whom did
I owe!—Lord! to whom did I owe!" I cannot tell, but I
know that I was in debt. It is a terrible thing, gentlemen,
to be in debt; speaking for myself, I have decided to die of
it.—And now what tortures me most of all is that I have
passed the debt on to you: to you, Cocles . . . Cocles!
Your eye does not belong to you, since the money with
which I gave it you did not belong to me. 'What hast
thou, that thou hast not received?' says the Scripture . . .
received from whom? from whom? ? from whom? ? ?—
My torment is unbearable."

The wretched man's voice came in fits and starts; it
was blurred and strangled by coughing, sobs and tears.
Prometheus and Cocles listened anxiously; they had taken
each other by the hand, and were shuddering. Damocles
said, as if he could see them:

"Duty is a terrible thing, gentlemen . . . but how much
more terrible is the remorse one feels for having wanted
to unburden oneself of a duty . . . As if a debt could be
any the less real, for being taken on someone else's
shoulders . . . But your eye is burning you, Cocles!—
Cocles! ! I'm sure your glass eye is burning you; pluck it
out!—If it doesn't burn you, then it ought to.—But
your eye doesn't belong to you . . . And if it doesn't
belong to you, then it belongs to your brother . . . It
belongs to whom? whom? ? whom? ? ?"

The poor man was weeping; he was gradually losing

his wits and his strength; sometimes he stared at Cocles
and Prometheus, seemed to recognize them, and cried out
to them:

"But understand me, for pity's sake! When I claim
your pity, I don't mean a cold compress on my forehead,
a glass of cold water, a hot drink; I want you to understand me. Help me to understand myself, for pity's sake!
I have this *thing*, which came to me from I don't know
where, and I owe it to whom? whom?? whom???—
and trying, one day, to cease to owe it, and thinking it
possible, I go and make gifts to others with this *thing*!
To others!!—to Cocles, the charity of an eye!! But that
eye doesn't belong to you, Cocles! Cocles!! Give it back.
Give it back to whom? to whom?? to whom???"

As they could bear it no longer, Cocles and Prometheus
left.

IV

"You see there," said Cocles, as he descended the stairs, "what happens to a man who gets rich on the suffering of another."

"Yes, but do you suffer?" asked Prometheus.

"Sometimes, with my eye," said Cocles, "but hardly any more from my slap in the face; the inflammation has gone down. And I wouldn't like not to have received it: it revealed my own goodness to me. It flatters me; I am well pleased with it. I never stop thinking that my pain gave a livelihood to my neighbour, and was worth five hundred francs to him."

"Yes, Cocles, but the neighbour is dying of it," said Prometheus.

"Didn't you tell him that a man must feed his eagle?— But what's the good! Damocles and I have never been able to understand each other; our points of view are diametrically opposite."

Prometheus took leave of Cocles, and hurried to the house of Zeus the banker.

"For pity's sake, show yourself!" he said; "or at least make yourself known to him. The poor wretch is dying in anguish. I can understand your killing him, as it gives you pleasure; but let him at least know Who is killing him—and then die in peace."

The Miglionaire replied: "I don't wish to lose my prestige."

V

Damocles made an admirable end; he uttered, a little before his last hour came, words of the kind that wring tears from the most hardened unbelievers, and make religious people say "How edifying!" His most note-worthy sentiment was the one that is so well expressed by these words: "I hope at least it won't have made him go short."

"Why, who?" everyone asked.

"*Him,*" said Damocles, breathing his last—"the one who gave me . . . whatever it was."

"Of course not!—it was the Good Lord Himself," rejoined the waiter, adroitly.

It was on these words of comfort that Damocles died.

THE FUNERAL

"Oh!" said Prometheus to Cocles, as they left the death-bed. "—All this is so horrible! The death of Damocles overwhelms me. Is it true that my lecture was the cause of his illness?"

"I can't swear to it," said the waiter, "but I do at least know that he was very much stirred by what you said about your eagle."

"Our eagle," corrected Cocles.

"I felt so convinced," said Prometheus.

"That's why you convinced him. . . . Your speech was extremely stimulating . . ."

"I thought no one was listening. . . . I stressed everything so. . . . If I'd known he was listening . . ."

"What would you have said?"

"The very same things," stammered Prometheus.

"Well, then!"

"But I wouldn't say them any more, now."

"Why, have you stopped being convinced?"

"Damocles was all too convinced. I have other ideas concerning my eagle."

"By the way, where is it?"

"You needn't worry, Cocles, I have my eye on it."

"Well, goodbye. I am going into mourning," said Cocles. "When shall we see each other again?"

"Why . . . at the funeral, I suppose. I shall give an address there," said Prometheus. "There's something I have to put right. And then, I invite you for afterwards; I'm giving the wake-feast, and it's to be in the very same restaurant where we saw Damocles for the first time."

VI

At the hour fixed for the funeral, there was no grea
crowd to be seen; Damocles was known to few; his deatl
passed unnoticed by all who took no interest in the fact
related in this story. Prometheus, the waiter and Cocle
met at the cemetery, where they were joined by a fev
idlers who had been present at the lecture. Everyone kep
his eyes on Prometheus; they knew he was going to
speak; they said to themselves: "What is he going to
say?"—for they remembered what he had said on th
previous occasion. But amazement preceded his speech
and was caused by the fact that no one could recogniz
him: he was plump, spruce and smiling; smiling to sucl
a degree that his conduct was thought hardly decen
when, still wreathed in smiles, he advanced to the edg
of the grave, and then, turning his back upon it, pro
nounced these simple words:

THE STORY OF TITYRUS

"Gentlemen, who so kindly deign to give me your attention, the words of the Scriptures which will serve as my text for to-day's brief discourse, are these:—
—*Let the dead bury the dead.*
So we need trouble ourselves no more about Damocles.
—The last time I saw you gathered together was when you had come to hear me talk about my eagle; Damocles died of it; let the dead, etc. . . . Still, it's because of him, or rather, it's thanks to his death, that I have now killed my eagle. . . ."

"Killed his eagle! ! !" they all exclaimed.

"And while we are on the subject, here is an anecdote. . . . Let's forget all I have just said."

"In the beginning was Tityrus.

And Tityrus, being alone, and completely surrounded by marshes, was lost in boredom.—Now Menalcas happened to pass by, and planted an idea in the brain of Tityrus, and a seed in the marsh before him. And this idea was the seed, and this seed was the Idea. And with the help of God the seed quickened and became a little plant, and Tityrus, morning and evening, falling on his knees before it, thanked God for giving it to him. And this plant grew, and as it had powerful roots, it had before long completely dried the earth around it, so that Tityrus had a plot of firm ground on which to set his feet, and rest his head, and fortify the work of his hands.

When this plant had reached the height of Tityrus, he was able to take some pleasure in sleeping outstretched beneath its shadow. Now this sapling, being an oak, was destined to grow enormously; so that very soon the work of Tityrus' hands sufficed no longer to weed and hoe the earth round the oak-tree, to water it, and lop it, and trim it, and prune it, and keep it free of caterpillars, and ensure in the fullness of the season a good crop of its fruits, which were as numerous as they were various. So he joined unto himself a weeder, a hoer, a waterer, a lopper, a trimmer, a pruner, a remover of caterpillars, and some boys to gather the fruit. And as each one of them had to confine himself strictly to his own speciality, there was some chance that the duty of each might be well done.

So that everyone could be paid regularly, Tityrus needed a book-keeper, who soon shared with a cashier the task of looking after Tityrus' fortune; and Tityrus' fortune waxed great like the oak-tree.

Certain disputes having arisen between the trimmer and the pruner as to the respective limits of their functions, Tityrus awoke to the necessity of having an arbitrator, who summoned two lawyers to sit beside him, one for, and one against; Tityrus hired a secretary to record their decisions, and as the sole purpose of recording them was to provide documentation for the future, they had to have a keeper of the records. Meanwhile, little by little, houses rose from the ground; and there had to be police for the streets, and safeguards against abuses.

Tityrus, overburdened with business, began to fall ill; he sent for a doctor, who advised him to get married—and as he could not suffice alone for the care of so many people, he was forced to choose a deputy, the consequence of which was that they elected Tityrus mayor. Henceforth he had all too little leisure left in which to fish from the windows of his house, which continued as before to open on the marshes.

Then Tityrus appointed holidays for the recreation of his people; but as their amusements were expensive, and none of them had a great deal of money, in order to lend to all, Tityrus began by taxing the income of each.

Now the oak-tree, in the midst of the plain (for in spite of the town, and in spite of the efforts of the multitude of men, that expanse had never succeeded in ceasing to be The Plain), this oak-tree, I repeat, in the midst of the plain, had no difficulty in being so situated that one of its sides was in the shade, and the other in the sun. Under this oak-tree then, on the shady side, Tityrus dispensed justice; on the sunny side, he performed his natural functions.

And Tityrus was happy, for he felt his life was useful to others, and excessively busy.

II

Human effort is cultivable. The activity of Tityrus seemed to grow with encouragement; his natural ingenuity suggesting fresh employments, he was seen to work with all his might at furnishing, papering and arranging his house. His choice of hangings, and the commodity of his household fittings, were much admired. He was industrious, and excelled in empiricism; he even invented a little set of hooks on lazy-tongs to hang his bath-sponges on the wall; but after three or four days ceased to find it at all convenient.

And Tityrus, next to his own room, had another built for the interests of the nation; the two rooms had the same entrance, by way of indicating that the two interests were the same; but owing to the common entrance, which provided the same ventilation for both rooms, the two chimneys could not draw together, and in cold weather, if there was fire in the one, there was smoke in the other. So on days when he wanted to have a fire, Tityrus made it his custom to open his window.

As Tityrus protected everything, and worked for the propagation of species, there came a time when slugs crawled in such abundance over his garden-walks that, for fear of squashing one, he didn't know where to set his foot, and finally resigned himself to going out less often.

He sent for a circulating library, with a lady librarian to issue the books, and he took out a subscription with her. As her name was Angela, he acquired the habit of going every other day to spend his evenings with her. It was in this way that Tityrus learned metaphysics, algebra and theodicy. Tityrus and Angela began, together and with much success, to cultivate various recreational forms of the fine arts; and, as Angela displayed a special taste for music, they hired a grand piano, on which she used to execute the little tunes he composed for her between visits.

Tityrus would say to Angela—"All these occupations will be the death of me: I can't go on; I'm feeling worn out; these solidarities with fellow-humanity activate my scruples; if they increase, I decrease. What shall I do?"

"Supposing we went away together?" said Angela.

"You might, but I can't: I have my oak-tree."

"Supposing you left it?" said Angela.

"Leave my oak-tree! How can you think of such a thing?"

"Isn't it nearly big enough to grow by itself?"

"Yes, but I'm attached to it."

"Detach yourself," replied Angela.

And soon afterwards, having at last realized that, all in all, his occupations and responsibilities and various scruples had no more power to hold him than the oak-tree, Tityrus smiled, spread his sails to the wind, and departed, taking with him the cash-box and Angela; and towards the end of the day, with her by his side, he walked down the boulevard that leads from the Madeleine to the Opéra.

III

That evening the boulevard wore a strange appearance. One felt that some unaccustomed and solemn event was in preparation. An enormous, serious, anxious crowd was jostling together, obstructing the pavement and almost overflowing on to the roadway, which long lines of police were having great trouble in keeping free. The terraces in front of the restaurants, disproportionately enlarged by the deployment of chairs and tables, made the obstruction more complete and rendered circulation impossible. Sometimes an impatient onlooker perched himself on top of a chair for a moment, just long enough for someone to ask him to get down. It was evident that everyone was waiting; one felt, without any possible doubt, that between the banks of the pavement, along the guarded roadway, something or other was about to descend. After succeeding with great difficulty in finding a table, and hiring it at a very high price, Angela and Tityrus took their seats in front of two glasses of beer and asked the waiter:

"What is everyone waiting for?"

"Where has Monsieur been all this time?" said the waiter. "Doesn't Monsieur know that they're waiting for Melibœus? He's due to pass between five and six o'clock . . . and there—listen: I believe you can already hear his flute."

From the far end of the boulevard rose the faint sound of a reed-pipe. The crowd grew more attentive still, and shuddered with anticipation. The sound grew louder and more near.

"Oh! How moving it is!" said Angela.

The declining sun darted its rays from one end of the boulevard to the other. And, as if issuing from the splendours of the sunset, they saw Melibœus at last advancing, preceded by the simple sound of his flute.

At first one could distinguish nothing clearly except his general demeanour, but when he drew nearer:

"Oh! How charming he is!" said Angela.

Melibœus, meanwhile, arriving in front of Tityrus, stopped playing his flute, halted abruptly, saw Angela, and everyone noticed that he was naked.

"Oh!" said Angela, leaning over Tityrus, "how handsome he is! How agile are his loins! How adorable is his fluting!"

Tityrus was a little embarrassed.

"Ask him where he is going," said Angela.

"Where are you going?" questioned Tityrus.

Melibœus replied: "*Eo Romam.*"

"What does he say?" Angela went on.

Tityrus: "You won't understand, my dear."

"But you will explain it to me," said Angela.

"*Romam,*" insisted Melibœus, "*—urbem quam dicunt Romam.*"

Angela: "Oh! What a delicious thing to say!—What does it mean?"

Tityrus: "But, my dear Angela, I assure you it isn't as delicious as all that; it means, purely and simply, that he is going to Rome."

"Rome!" said Angela pensively—"Oh! How I would love to see Rome!"

Meliboeus, taking his pipe again, began once more his primitive melody. At this sound Angela excitedly sat up, rose and drew near; Meliboeus crooked his elbow, and she took his arm, and the two of them, continuing in this way along the boulevard, receded, dissolved, vanished in the definitive twilight.

Then the unleashed multitude was agitated in violent tumult. On every side one heard questioning voices:— "What did he say?" "What did he do?" "Who was that woman?" And when, a few moments later, the evening papers appeared, a wild curiosity carried every copy away as in a cyclone; and suddenly everyone learned that the woman was Angela, and this Meliboeus was someone without any clothes who was going to Italy.

And then, all its curiosity subsiding, the crowd flowed away like running water, leaving the boulevards deserted. —And Tityrus found himself once more alone and completely surrounded by marshes.

Let's forget all I have just said.

For a few moments irrepressible laughter shook the audience.

"Gentlemen, I am glad that my story amuses you," said Prometheus, joining in the laughter. "Since the death of Damocles, I have discovered the secret of laughter.—And now, I have finished, gentlemen; we had better let the dead bury the dead, and go at once to have our luncheon."

He took the waiter by one arm, Cocles by the other; everyone left the cemetery. The rest of the assembly passed through the gates and dispersed.

"Excuse me," said Cocles, "your story was charming, and you amused us extremely . . . but I didn't quite grasp its relevance . . ."

"If it had had more relevance, you wouldn't have laughed so much," said Prometheus; "don't expect to find too much sense in all that;—my chief wish was to divert you, and I'm glad to have succeeded; didn't I owe you as much? I'd bored you so fearfully the other time."

They regained the boulevards.

"Where are we going?" said the waiter.

"To your restaurant, if you don't mind, in memory of our first meeting."

"You're just passing it," said the waiter.

"I don't recognize your window."

"That's because we have a brand-new one, now."

"I was forgetting that my eagle . . . Have no fear: it will never do it again."

"Then what you were saying," said Cocles, "is really true?"

"What?"

"That you have killed it?"

"And that we are going to eat it . . . Can you doubt it?" said Prometheus: "haven't you looked at me yet? Did I ever dare to laugh, in its time? Wasn't I appallingly thin?"

"Certainly, you were."

"It had been eating me for long enough; I decided it was my turn.—Let's begin! Come along! Let's begin, gentlemen!—Waiter . . . don't serve us: as a last tribute to the memory of Damocles, sit in his place."

The meal was more hilarious than it is permissible to relate here, and everyone thought the eagle delicious. At dessert they all drank its health.

"So it won't have been good for anything?" they asked.

"Don't say that, Cocles!—Its flesh has nourished us.—
When I asked it a question, it wouldn't answer . . . But
I eat it with no feeling of animosity; if it had made me
suffer less, it would have been less plump; if it had been
less plump, it would have been less delectable."

"What remains of its beauty of yesterday?"

"I have kept all its feathers."

*It is with a pen made from one of them that I have written
this little book. May you succeed, rare friend, in finding it not
so bad as it might be.*

EPILOGUE

BY WAY OF TRYING TO MAKE THE READER BELIEVE
THAT IF THIS BOOK IS WHAT IT IS
IT IS NOT THE FAULT OF THE AUTHOR

One doesn't write the books one wishes.
—Goncourt Journal.

THE STORY OF Leda had raised such a stir, and covered Tyndarus with such glory, that Minos was not unduly distressed when Pasiphaë came and said to him: "It can't be helped, dear. I simply don't care for men."

But later she said: "It's too provoking (and it wasn't any too easy, I assure you!). I hoped there was a hidden god in him.— If Zeus had had anything to do with it, I should have given birth to a Heavenly Twin; thanks to this animal, I've brought into the world nothing but a moon-calf."

REFLECTIONS

I

What in agriculture is called rotation of crops, in man is called circular madness.

II

As soon as a man has an idea he writes a whole book, not so much in order to explain it, as to excuse himself for having had it.

III

When one studies the problem of the purpose of a work of art, one discovers in the end that the justification, the symbol of the work, is its *design*.

A well-designed work is necessarily symbolic; around what could its various parts come to group themselves? what could guide their ordering? if not the idea of the work, which carries out this symbolic order.

A work of art is an idea which one exaggerates.

A symbol is that around which a book is designed.

A sentence is an excrescence on an idea.

181

IV

All things are in a state of perpetual disequilibrium—hence their transitoriness.

Equilibrium is a condition of perfect "health"; what Taine calls a happy accident—but it is unrealizable in the material world for the reason we have just mentioned; it is realizable only in a work of art.—A work of art is an extra-temporal equilibrium, an artificial state of health.

V

I maintain that what an artist has to believe in is this: that there is a special world, to which he alone has the key. It's not that he must contribute *something* new, though even that would be an enormous achievement; but that *everything* in him must be or seem new, transmitted through a powerfully colouring idiosyncrasy.

He must have a *particular* philosophy, aesthetic, morality; his whole work tends only to show it. And that is what makes his style. He must also have a *particular* *wit*—his own *sense of fun*.

VI

Theory of the Book:—a dead letter?—A bag of seed.

VII

"This island, called Savu by the natives, is little known."
CAPTAIN COOK.

If it wasn't known at all, it wouldn't have a name.

What a *strange* habit men have of christening bits of land—and this island of all places! They only christen it on the day they think of leaving it—and they do so for the benefit of *others*.

VIII

Inertia of matter. Its passivity before it is traversed by an idea.

Elasticity! The worst of all inertias! Hypocrisy of immoveable matter; it seems to give way, makes you think victory is won and your effort ended, but springs back as soon as you let go; it was only inertia postponed; matter apparently plastic, which lends itself to exhausting our efforts. What stupid faculty of memory do you come to prove, after we had modelled you so closely to our taste, when you return to redispose yourself in your original outlines, which we were so anxious to forget—which we shall therefore never be able to forget. Elasticity!—matter's brute memory, inertia postponed, apparent docility. . . .

Elasticity is all around us; what in the immaterial world we call retroaction is nothing more—but with infinite complications—till matter becomes completely impregnated with it, completely changed by it.

Rejoinder: infinite receptivity of matter—porosity.

IX

The social problem?—by all means. But the moral problem is antecedent to it.

Man is more interesting than men; it is he, and not they, that God made in His image. Each is more valuable than all.

X

Synthesis must be preceded by analysis; and analysis, vital need of the intellect, springs from the feeling of complexity. The feeling of complexity can become a passionate amazement.

XI

Everything that has taken place in us, even if it was only once, can recur, given the help of time, given the silence of the will.

The only thing you can be sure of never doing is the thing you are sure of never understanding. Assurance of virtue annoys me, because it rests on incomprehension— I'm not talking about mental intelligence, which is merely logical, and understands nothing but relations between signs—I've no use for it. You understand only that which you are capable of doing; just as objects in nature only vibrate at the approach of a sound when they themselves, given the impact, are capable of producing it. And I don't say they ever will produce it—but thence often comes their indulgence, excuse of a future possibility.

Nil humanum a me alienum puto.

"There are no crimes so great that I haven't felt myself sometimes capable of committing them," says Goethe. The greatest intellects are also the most capable of great crimes, which ordinarily they don't commit, out of wisdom, love, and because they would be limited thereby.

XII

Doctrine of sin: being capable of all evil not to do any of it, and that's what good is; negative will—no, I don't like that. I like blindness towards evil to come from being dazzled by good; otherwise virtue is ignorance—poverty.

XIII

I can no more be grateful to "God" for creating me—than I could bear Him a grudge for my not existing, if I didn't exist.

XIV

Et sic Deus—semel jussit, semper paret.

God—Who keeps faith.—Miracles are God's acts of disobedience.

XV

Wanting to prove that *God exists*, is as absurd as to assert that He does not.

For our assertions and our proofs won't create Him . . . . . nor will they suppress Him.

XVI

I prefer to say that: the moment something exists, it's God. The explanation is of no use to me; He Himself explains Himself through the whole of Nature; that is His way of existing.

XVII

Prayer is the oratorical form of the soul.

XVIII

It is preposterous to believe that man needs tradition or history to understand an eternal God. The history of God can only be the history of what men have believed.

John the Baptist is the oratorical precaution of Christ.

XIX
I have always found my happiness in simplifying everything by progressively broader generalizations—so as to make my possession as veritably portable as the cup with which Hafiz caroused.

XX
Give consideration henceforth in each creature only to the unique and *different* part of which this common matter was merely the all too massive pedestal.

XXI
Paganism will only bring peace in so far as one assumes the existence above all these rival deities of a single power to dominate them.

It is in the feeling of concord, not of rivalry, that happiness consists; and even if all the forces of nature fought each one against all the rest, it is impossible for me not to conceive of a superior unity, presiding over this very struggle, prior to every division, in which each soul can take refuge for its well-being.

XXII
One ought never to buy anything except with love. Anybody and anything ought always to belong to the one who loves him or it best. Bread to the hungriest—the tit-bit to the one who prefers it, or who has already eaten. Such is the explanation of the drunkenness of the common people: they drink to forget that they do not possess what they desire; moreover, the drunkenness of

the upper classes is to be explained in the same manner. Drunkenness is never anything but a substitute for happiness. It is the acquisition of the dream of a thing, when one hasn't the money that commands the material acquisition of the thing dreamed of. The bottle that confers drunkenness is as good as a wishing-cap so long as one remains drunk. The terrible thing is that one can never get sufficiently tipsy.

XXIII

. . . He thought: the world might have had a different history. The surface of the earth might have been otherwise covered. If the world had never had any other inhabitants but creatures like myself, the world would have had no history.—I always hate careers that owe their existence only to the malignity of men.

XXIV

In all this comedy—with the important acts—birth and death—at its two extremities—we haven't begun to perceive the one; we have ceased to perceive the other. One is even forced to believe that, as soon as the handful of earth is thrown on the grave, we cease to be aware that we are dead. One only perceives the death of other people—because it facilitates our life.

XXV

Individual characters are more generalized (I mean more human) than racial characters. One must realize: man, as an individual, tries to evade his race. And as soon as he ceases to represent his race, he represents mankind; idiosyncrasy is a pretext for generalizations.

XXVI

RIGHTEOUSNESS. All that this word implies.

XXVII

The strange mental cowardice which makes us perpetually doubt whether future happiness can equal past happiness is often our only cause for misery; we cling to the phantoms of our bereavements as if we were in duty bound to prove to others the reality of our sorrow. We search after memories and wreckage, we would like to live the past over again, and we want to reiterate our joys long after they are drained to the dregs.

I hate every form of sadness, and cannot understand why trust in the beauty of the future should not prevail over worship of the past.

Isn't it like resembling those natives of the seashore who weep every evening for the sun foundered in the sea—and are still crying after the sunset long after the rejuvenated sun behind them has risen again?

XXVIII

". . . 'To suffer, or to die.'—*Aut pati aut mori*. You owe it to your audience to understand steadfastly all the force of this saying; . . . you will confess as I do that it contains in epitome the whole doctrine of the Son of Man and the whole spirit of Christianity."

And further on: "No two things can be more opposite than to live in accordance with nature and to live in accordance with grace."

BOSSUET: *Panegyric on Saint Teresa.*

Too bad.

XXIX

"The self is odious" . . . you say.

. . . Mine isn't.

I would have loved it in someone else; am I to turn up my nose at it just because it's my own?

On what worse self might I not have happened! (To start with, I'm alive and that's magnificent.)

I'm sorry for you if you feel in yourself anything to hate. All I hate is this dismal ethic; if I love my *self*, don't think I love yours any the less, or that it's because of any more or less of happiness.

(But you're alive too, I suppose, and that is magnificent too.)

XXX

The history of man is the history of the truths man has set free.

I don't mean, you understand, when I say this, to consider truths as a small number of elect whose liber-ation, or rather election, is a manner of recognizing their right of kingship over ourselves. So that their liberty would be bought at the price of ours.

No.—Let us reject even this word Truth—which would lead people to believe too easily that the despotism of certain Ideas is legitimate. Let us say, not Truths, but Ideas.—And let us call Ideas every perception of a relationship; or, if you like, metaphorically, every re-fraction within the human brain of the relationship that effects it. The number of Ideas is as infinite as the number of relationships, or nearly so.

I like, in order not to suppress for myself every reason for existing or for being glad to exist—to consider man-kind as the putting into effect of possible relationships. The almost infinity of possible relationships assures for mankind an almost infinite duration. The relationships that have been effectuated constitute the history of the past.—That's a thing that's over and done with, and, whether the game was well, or badly played, there's no point in going back to it—besides, we couldn't if we tried. The least of to-day's ideas could not exist without yesterday's almost infinite play of relationships. So that now we've got rid of them at last!

It is in this way that little by little mankind sets itself free. But so little that it never notices.

But all the same don't let this make you go and believe in progress, unless for the following reason:

No movement whatsoever, even that of a crab, can be imagined as being otherwise than forward; and even if you turned all your faces towards it, the past would recede none the less into the past. What's done cannot be done again; pleonasm is impossible here.

But to believe that mankind can find a goal outside itself, and one not projected by itself, would be sheer folly and chasing after one's shadow. Man's progress is only within himself, and hasn't the victorious signific-ance you think.

Ossa piled on Pelion collapses, and heaven can't be taken by storm—and besides, one wouldn't find there the little band of Truths, sitting on thrones and leaving corners for us to sit down too.

The gods, if they existed, would see our interminable labour as children at the seaside find entertainment in the relative progresses of the waves. A wave advances; O progress! it rises; it covers the shore, it drowns every-thing—it leaves its foam behind and is gone; another takes its place and rises a little higher—O progress! it's the rising tide; the tide goes out; next day it gains yet a few more inches of seashore—O progress! how far will it not go to-morrow? But the day after to-morrow the spring tides are over and the sea ebbs—but continues its work nevertheless, and gradually eats away the land.

Time and space are the trestles of the platform the innumerable truths have set up, with the aid of our minds, to stage their play—and we act our parts on it like willing, convinced, devoted and voluptuous marionettes. I don't see anything in this to be sorry about, for I on the con-trary take pleasure in this conviction of *my* role, and this role after all, if it's motivated by everything, is neverthe-less invented by each man for himself.

You will learn to consider humanity as the staging of ideas on the earth.

XXXI

Our only value is a representative one.

They were oppressed by the burden of themselves, and didn't know what to do to get rid of it. Charity didn't tempt them in the least. The individual became unbearable to them, and others still more than themselves. If they were tired of paying attention to themselves, it certainly wasn't so that they could pay attention to others.—But to what could they pay attention, after that? What could they take up with?

This tormented them to such a degree, that they thought ideas were subordinate to men. But as soon as they realized ideas were sovereign, they paid attention to nothing but them, and in them forgot themselves.

XXXII

Things have need of us in order to exist, or to feel that they exist, and, without us, remain in a state of waiting. And hence man feels an anxious uneasiness: the pressure in us of all that has not yet been and wishes to be—of all the unknown that asks for its little moment of thought, seems to entreat us for existence, because everything has to go that way—and as if there were some joy in telling oneself that one has been—when one is no longer.

XXXIII

It is easy to regard the soul as like this patch of ground, on which many diverse plants grow and such multitudes of insects live. There's overcrowding; there's struggle; so there will be suppression. It's too much! It's too much; if you don't pull anything up, nature will take charge of the struggle.—So much the better!